Thomas

Stephen Lucius Gwynn

Alpha Editions

This edition published in 2023

ISBN : 9789357948548

Design and Setting By
Alpha Editions
www.alphaedis.com
Email - info@alphaedis.com

Contents

CHAPTER I
BOYHOOD AND EARLY POEMS

Sudden fame, acquired with little difficulty, suffers generally a period of obscuration after the compelling power which attaches to a man's living personality has been removed; and from this darkness it does not always emerge. Of such splendour and subsequent eclipse, Moore's fate might be cited as the capital example.

The son of a petty Dublin tradesman, he found himself, almost from his first entry on the world, courted by a brilliant society; each year added to his friendships among the men who stood highest in literature and statesmanship; and his reputation on the Continent was surpassed only by that of Scott and Byron. He did not live to see a reaction. Lord John Russell could write boldly in 1853, a year after his friend's death, that "of English lyrical poets, Moore is surely the greatest." There is perhaps no need to criticise either this attitude of excessive admiration, or that which in many cases has replaced it, of tolerant contempt. But it is as well to emphasise at the outset the fact that even to-day, more than a century after he began to publish, Moore is still one of the poets most popular and widely known throughout the English-speaking world. His effect on his own race at least has been durable; and if it be a fair test of a poet's vitality to ask how much of his work could be recovered from oral tradition, there are not many who would stand it better than the singer of the Irish Melodies. At least the older generation of Irishmen and Irishwomen now living have his poetry by heart.

The purpose of this book is to give, if possible, a just estimate of the man's character and of his work as a poet. The problem, so far as the biographical part is concerned, is not to discover new material but to select from masses already in print. The Memoirs of his Life, edited by Lord John Russell, fill eight volumes, though the life with which they deal was neither long nor specially eventful. In addition we have allusions to Moore, as a widely known social personage, in almost every memoir of that time; and newspaper references by thousands have been collected. These extraneous sources, however, add very little to the impression which is gained by a careful reading of the correspondence and of the long diaries in which Moore's nature, singularly unsecretive, displays itself with perfect frankness. Whether one's aim be to justify Moore or to condemn him, the most effective means are provided by his own words; and for nearly everything that I have to allege in the narrative part of this work, Moore, himself is the authority. Nor is the critical estimate which has to be put forward, though remote from that of Moore's official biographer, at all unlike that which the poet himself seems to have formed of his work.

Thomas Moore was born in Dublin on the 28th of May 1779, at No. 12 Aungier Street, where his father, a native of Kerry, kept a grocer's shop. His mother, Anastasia Clodd, was the daughter of a small provision merchant in Wexford. Moore was their eldest child, and of the brothers and sisters whom he mentions, only two girls, his sisters Katherine and Ellen, appear to have grown up or to have played any part in his life. His parents were evidently prosperous people, devoted to their clever boy and ambitious to secure him social promotion by giving scope to the talents which he showed from his early schooldays. The memoir of his youth, which Moore wrote in middle life, notes the special pleasure which his mother took in the friendship of a certain Miss Dodd, an elderly maiden lady moving in "a class of society somewhat of a higher level than ours"; and it is easy enough to understand why the precocious imp of a boy found favour with this distinguished person and her guests. He had all the gifts of an actor and a mimic, and they were encouraged in him first at home, and then at the boarding-school to which he was sent. Samuel Whyte, its head master, had been the teacher of Sheridan, and though he discovered none of Sheridan's abilities, the connection with the Sheridan family, added to his own tastes, had brought him into close touch with the stage. He was the author of a didactic poem on "The Theatre," a great director of private theatricals, and a teacher of elocution. Such a man was not likely to neglect the gifts of the clever small boy entrusted to him, and Master Moore, at the age of eleven, already figured on the playbill of some important private theatricals as reciting the Epilogue. He was encouraged also in the habit of rhyming, a habit that reached back as far as he could remember; and before his fifteenth year was far gone, he attained to the honours of print in a creditable magazine, the *Anthologia Hibernica*. The first of his contributions was an amatory address to a Miss Hannah Byrne, herself, it appears, a poetess. The lines, "To Zelia on her charging the Author with writing too much on love," need not be quoted (though the subject is characteristic), nor the "Pastoral Ballad" which followed in the number for October 1793. It is worth noting, however, that in 1794 we find Moore paraphrasing Anacreon's Fifth Ode; and further that in March of the same year he is acknowledging his debt to Mr. Samuel Whyte with verses beginning

"Hail heaven-taught votary of the laurel'd Nine"

—an unusual form of address from a schoolboy to his pedagogue.

Briefly, one gathers the impression that Moore's schooldays were enlivened by many small gaieties, while his holidays abounded with the same distractions. The family was sent down to Sandymount, now a suburb, but then a seaside village on Dublin Bay, and there, in addition to sea-bathing, they had their fill of mild play-acting. Moore reproduces some lines from an epilogue written for one of these occasions when the return to school was imminent:—

"Our Pantaloon that did so agéd look
Must now resume his youth, his task, his book;
Our Harlequin who skipp'd, leap'd, danced, and died,
Must now stand trembling by his tutor's side."

And he notes genially how the pathos of his farewell nearly moved him to tears as he recited the closing words—doubtless with a thrilling - tremble in his accents. é Moore was always ἀρτιδακρύς. But he was a healthy, active youngster, and we read that he emulated Harlequin in jumping talents, as well as in the command of tears and laughter; and practised over the rail of a tent-bed till he could at last "perform the headforemost leap of his hero most successfully."

School made little break in these pleasures; for while the family were at the seaside, his indulgent father provided the boy with a pony on which he rode down every Saturday to stay over the Sunday; "and at the hour when I was expected, there generally came my sister with a number of young girls to meet me, and full of smiles and welcomes, walked by the side of my pony into the town." Never was a boy more petted. About this time, too, his musical gifts began to be discovered; for Mrs. Moore insisted that her daughter Katherine should be taught not only the harpsichord, but also the piano, and that a piano should be bought. On this instrument Moore taught himself to play; and since his mother had a pleasant voice and a talent for giving gay little supper-parties, musical people used to come to the house, and the boy had plenty of chances for showing off his accomplishments, accompanying himself, and developing already his uncanny knack of dramatic singing.

A young gentleman thus brought up was, one would say, in a fair way to be spoiled, and Moore, looking back, is quick to recognise the danger. Yet he is fully justified in the comment which closes his narrative of the triumphant entries into Sandymount with schoolgirls escorting his pony:—

> "There is far more of what is called vanity in my now reporting the tribute, than I felt then in receiving it; and I attribute very much to the cheerful and kindly circumstances which thus surrounded my childhood, that spirit of enjoyment and, I may venture to add, good temper, which has never, thank God, failed me to the present time (July 1833)."

Moreover, if his parents were interested in his pleasures, they were no less concerned about his work. His mother, he writes, examined him daily in his studies; sometimes even, when kept out late at a party, she would wake the boy out of his sleep in the small hours of morning, and bid him sit up and repeat over his lessons. Her affectionate care met with that return from her son which was continued to the end of her life. There was nothing in his power that Moore would not do to please his mother.

Nevertheless, touching as the relation was, it had its weak side, and Moore in time realised it. In a notable passage of his diary, which describes the pleasant days spent by him at Abbotsford in 1825, we read how he congratulated Scott on the advantages of his upbringing—the open-air life, field sports, and free intercourse with the peasantry.

> "I said that the want of this manly training showed itself in my poetry, which would perhaps have had a far more vigorous character, if it had not been for the sort of *boudoir* education I had received." ("The only thing, indeed," he adds, "that conduced to brace and invigorate my mind was the strong political feelings that were stirring round me when I was a boy, and in which I took a deep and most ardent interest.")

Part of this stirring manifested itself in a secret association under John Moore's own roof; for the son had organised his father's two clerks into a debating and literary society, of which he constituted himself president. The meetings took place after the common meal of the household was over, when the clerks retired to their bedroom, and Master Thomas to his own apartment—a corner of the same bedroom, but boarded off, fitted with a table, chest of drawers, and book-case, and decorated by its owner with inscriptions of his own composition "in the manner, as I flattered myself, of Shenstone at the Leasowes." The secret society met at dead of night in a closet beyond the large bedroom, once or twice a week; and each member was bound to produce a riddle or rebus in verse, which the others were set to solve. And in addition to this more literary part of the proceedings, the members discussed politics—Tom Ennis, the senior clerk, being a strong nationalist.

Politics certainly played a great part in moulding Moore's feelings and imagination, and it should be observed that his nonage almost coincided with the duration of Ireland's independent Parliament. He was three years old when the Volunteers established the freedom of the legislature in College Green, and twenty-one when Pitt and Castlereagh purchased its extinction. His father, as a Catholic, had naturally a keen interest in the great question of reform and Catholic enfranchisement, and Moore remembered being taken by him to a dinner in honour of Napper Tandy, when the hero of the evening noticed the small boy. The Latin usher at Whyte's school too, Mr. Donovan, was an ardent patriot, and in the hours of special instruction which he devoted to the young scholar—for Moore had early outstripped his class-fellows in Latin and Greek—he taught his pupil more than the classics. But these influences bred at most a predisposition. It was Trinity College that made Moore a rebel—or as nearly a rebel as he ever became.

The measure of partial enfranchisement passed in 1793 admitted Catholics to study in the University of Dublin, though its emoluments were denied them. A curious point should be noted here. The entry under June 2, 1794, reads: "Thomas Moore, P. Prot," *i.e.* Commoner (pensionarius), Protestant. Now Moore himself states that it was for a while debated in the family circle whether he should be entered as a Protestant to qualify him for scholarship, fellowship and the rest; he does not seem to know that a preliminary step was actually taken, quite possibly by his school-master. John Moore's political friends were mostly Protestant ("the Catholics," his son writes, "being still too timorous to come forward openly in their own cause"); the atmosphere into which the student entered was strongly Protestant, the friends whom he made were of the dominant religion. But neither then nor at any time was Moore prepared to change creeds for material advantage. This is the more remarkable because the family's religion was none of the strictest. Moore notes that while at college he abandoned the practice of confession, his mother, after some protest, "very wisely consenting."

Whether owing to the lack of incentive, or because he had no taste for science, then a necessary part of any honours course, Moore troubled little about academic successes, and, after gaining a single premium in his first year, decided to "confine himself to such parts of the course as fell within his own tastes and pursuits." Incidentally he earned distinction for a composition in English verse sent in instead of the prescribed Latin prose; and, needless to say, was busy with less authorised verse-writing. He did, however, in his third year, 1797, present himself for the scholarship examination and was (he says) placed on the list of successful candidates, though his religion disqualified him for enjoyment of the privileges. Records show that on Tuesday, 13th June of that year, thirteen exhibitions were given, supplementary to the list of scholars published on Trinity Monday (the 12th), and on this list Moore stands first. The award was presumably a solatium.

But the serious and lasting part of his university education was gained, as so often happens, not from his tutors but from his associates. The recall of Lord Fitzwilliam in March 1795—"that fatal turning-point in Irish history," as Mr. Lecky calls it—had shattered the hopes of Irish Catholics and made civil war a result to be eagerly urged by extremists on both sides. "The political ferment soon found its way within the walls of our university," writes Moore; and among his personal friends was a young man destined to tragic fame.

"This youth was Robert Emmet, whose brilliant success in his college studies, and more particularly in the scientific portion of them, had crowned his career, as far as he had gone, with all the honours of the course; while his powers of oratory displayed at a debating society, of which, about this time (1796-7), I became a member, were beginning to excite universal attention, as well from the eloquence as the political boldness of his displays. He was, I rather think, by two classes, my senior, though it might have been only by one. But there was, at all events, such an interval between our standings as, at that time of life, makes a material difference; and when I became a member of the debating society, I found him in full fame, not only for his scientific attainments but also for the blamelessness of his life and the grave suavity of his manners."

In the beginning of 1797 this debating club came to an end, and Emmet as well as Moore transferred his energies to the more important Historical Society. Here Moore, by his own account, distinguished himself only as the author of "a burlesque poem called an 'Ode upon Nothing, with Notes by Trismegistus Rustifustius,'" which earned first a medal by general acclamation, and then a vote of censure by reason of the broad licence of certain passages. Emmet, however, was a member of a different kind, and the speeches delivered by him attracted so much attention that a senior man was detailed by the governing Board to attend meetings and answer the young orator. About the same time a paper called *The Press* was set up by Emmet's elder brother, Thomas Addis Emmet, and other leaders of the United Irishmen; and in this Moore published anonymously a "Letter to the Students of Trinity College." The letter was, by Moore's account of it, treasonable enough, and when, according to custom, he read out the paper to his father and mother at home, they pronounced it to be "very bold." Next day a friend called and made some veiled allusion to the matter, which Moore's mother caught at, and she, says Moore, "most earnestly entreated of me never again to venture on so dangerous a step." Her son promised, and a few days later Emmet's influence was added to the mother's. Moore's account of the circumstance is so characteristic that it must be quoted.

"A few days after, in the course of one of those strolls into the country which Emmet and I used often to take together, our conversation turned upon this letter, and I gave him to understand it was mine; when, with that almost feminine gentleness of manner which he possessed, and which is so often found in such determined spirits, he owned to me that on reading the letter, though pleased with its contents, he could not help regretting that the public attention had been thus drawn to the politics of the University, as it might have the effect of awakening the vigilance of the college authorities, and frustrate the progress of the good work (as we both considered it) which was going on there so quietly. Even then, boyish as my own mind was, I could not help being struck with the manliness of the view which I saw he took of what men ought to do in such times and circumstances, namely, not to *talk* or *write* about their intentions, but to *act*. He had never before, I think, in conversation with me, alluded to the existence of the United Irish societies in college, nor did he now, or at any subsequent time, make any proposition to me to join in them, a forbearance which I attribute a good deal to his knowledge of the watchful anxiety about me which prevailed at home, and his foreseeing the difficulty which I should experience—from being, as the phrase is, constantly 'tied to my mother's apron-strings'—in attending the meetings of the society without being discovered."

It will be seen that Moore makes no claim for heroic conduct. One may assume with great certainty that in such a matter Emmet would not have obeyed a mother's injunctions. But although Moore's parents desired that their son should not go out of his way to incur risks, they were by no means of opinion that he should seek safety at any price. In 1797, on the eve of the rebellion, an inquisition was held within Trinity by Lord Chancellor FitzGibbon. On the first day of the tribunal's sitting, one of Emmet's friends, named Hamilton, refused to answer certain questions, and was sent down with the sentence of banishment from the University, carrying with it exclusion from all the learned professions. Moore went home and discussed the situation that evening.

> "The deliberate conclusion which my dear, honest father and mother came to was that, overwhelming as the consequences were to all their prospects and hopes for me, yet if the questions leading to the crimination of others which had been put to almost all examined on that day, and which poor Dacre Hamilton alone refused to answer, should be put also to me, I must in the same manner and at all risks return a similar refusal."

Next day Moore was called, and, after objecting to the oath, took it with the express reservation that he should refuse to answer any question which might criminate his associates. No such question was asked, and his fortitude was not put to the proof, nor does it seem that after this Moore dabbled in rebellion. Five years later, in 1803, when Emmet's abortive rising was nipped in the bud and the young leader went to his death, Moore was in London, preparing to depart for Bermuda. None of the letters preserved from that time contain any reference to this tragedy; but Moore's writings show again and again that the capacity for hero-worship was evoked in him by this friend of boyhood as by no other figure of his time. In the first number of the *Irish Melodies*, published in 1808, an early place is given to the lyric:—

"O breathe not his name, let it sleep in the shade,
Where cold and unhonoured his ashes are laid;
Sad, silent, and dark be the tears that we shed,
As the night-dew that falls on the grass o'er his head.

"But the night-dew that falls, though in silence it weeps,
Shall brighten with verdure the grave where he sleeps;
And the tear that we shed, though in secret it rolls,
Shall long keep his memory green in our souls."

Every one, in Ireland at least, who read these lines heard in them an echo of the closing passage in Emmet's speech from the dock:—

"I have but one request to ask at my departure from this world. It is the charity of its silence. Let no man write my epitaph. When my country shall have taken her place among the nations of the earth, then, and not till then, let my epitaph be written."

Emmet's words are established among the scriptures of the Irish people; but it may well be allowed that their fame would be less had not Moore caught up and amplified their thought with all his habitual felicity and more than his habitual passion. Nor is this all. "The Fire Worshippers" is the most characteristic of the four long poems set in the framework of *Lalla Rookh*, and "The Fire Worshippers" is a glorification of rebellion, which is merely made explicit in the following fine passage:—

"Rebellion! foul, dishonouring word,
Whose wrongful blight so oft has stain'd
The holiest cause that tongue or sword
Of mortal ever lost or gain'd,
How many a spirit, born to bless,
Hath sunk beneath that withering name,
Whom but a day's, an hour's success,
Had wafted to eternal fame!"

More than that, the rebels glorified are men like Emmet, who take up arms as a supreme protest, almost without hope of success.

"Who, though they know the strife is vain,
Who, though they know the riven chain
Snaps but to enter in the heart
Of him who rends its links apart,
Yet dare the issue,—blest to be
Even for one bleeding moment free,
And die in pangs of liberty!"

The affinity is not only between Emmet and the rebel hero Hafed. Hinda, the beloved of Hafed, has many traits that recall Emmet's betrothed, the beautiful and most unhappy Sarah Curran. For although John Philpot Curran was a leading supporter of Grattan's principles, yet no man more bitterly denounced Emmet's attempt; and Al Hassan himself, the fierce Moslem chief, could not have dealt more harshly with Hinda, had he detected her love for the Gheber, than did Curran when he was confronted with the proofs that his daughter continued her affection to a declared rebel. It is not hard to guess of whom Moore thought when he wrote the moving and beautiful lines which describe Hinda's passion in the days after her lover had been revealed to her for the foe of her father's arms:—

"Ah! not the love that should have bless'd
So young, so innocent a breast;
Not the pure, open, prosperous love,
That, pledged on earth and seal'd above,
Grows in the world's approving eyes,
In friendship's smile and home's caress,
Collecting all the heart's sweet ties
Into one knot of happiness!
No, Hinda, no—thy fatal flame
Is nursed in silence, sorrow, shame.—
A passion, without hope or pleasure,
In thy soul's darkness buried deep,
It lies, like some ill-gotten treasure,—
Some idol, without shrine or name,
O'er which its pale-eyed votaries keep
Unholy watch, while others sleep!"

Hafed and Hinda are lovers who find themselves united by all the attraction of their natures, yet separated irretrievably by external circumstances which are, in no small part, of the hero's making. The man is resolute to forfeit, not only life, but the fruition of declared love, sooner than abandon a national cause, even when that cause is most desperate;—the girl sees herself with "a divided duty," torn away by imperious love from all her natural loyalties;—and such lovers also, in Moore's own youth, were Robert Emmet and Sarah Curran. I have quoted the famous lyric in which he consecrates the memory of the man who died for the faith that was in him. Not less famous, and still more beautiful, is the melody which preserves the memory of the surviving lover, and the sad moods of retrospect which were evident in her broken life. Here, more than perhaps in any other poem, Moore has fixed in his words that plangent quality of voice, by which a hundred times he moved listeners to tears.

"She is far from the land where her young hero sleeps,
And lovers are round her sighing;
But coldly she turns from their gaze, and weeps,
For her heart in his grave is lying.

"She sings the wild song of her dear native plains,
Every note which he loved awaking:—
Ah! little they think, who delight in her strains,
How the heart of the Minstrel is breaking.

"He had lived for his love, for his country he died,
They were all that to life had entwin'd him;
Nor soon shall the tears of his country be dried,
Nor long will his love stay behind him.

"Oh! make her a grave where the sunbeams rest
When they promise a glorious morrow;
They'll shine o'er her sleep, like a smile from the West,
From her own loved island of sorrow."

With the terrible events of 1798 Moore had no personal concern. His memoir notes that he was ill in bed when the long-expected revolt broke out, and when folks in Dublin were scared by the going out of all the street lamps on the night fixed for an attempt on the metropolis. Yet it is strange how little trace is left in his writings by that bloodstained year. Even in his Life of Lord Edward Fitzgerald, we seem to find the result of subsequent reading and inquiry, rather than the narrative of one who was almost a man grown when Lord Edward's tragic end moved pity throughout the whole kingdom.

And in truth, though politics were always well to the front among Moore's interests, they never dominated his life. The memoir of his youth notes that even among his political associates other enthusiasms were cultivated. Edward Hudson, one of the Committee of United Irishmen, seized just before the rebellion broke out, was, Moore says, "passionately devoted to

Irish music," and had "collected and transcribed all our most beautiful airs." To intercourse with him in these days the poet ascribed much of his own early acquaintance with the chief source of his inspiration. Further, Moore formally completed his education by graduating in 1798, and before this time he had been entered at the Middle Temple by the father of his friend Beresford Burston, a young man of good family and of sporting tastes. But, while still an undergraduate, he had already commenced the composition whose success was to turn him from all serious thoughts of the bar.

The interest of another friend had procured him admission at all seasons to Marsh's Library, and here he plunged deep in miscellaneous reading. We read in the preface to his early volume, *Poetical Works of the late Thomas Little*, that "Mr. Little" (the supposititious author) "gave much of his time to the study of the amatory writers"; and it is safe to conclude that Mr. Little's original read, in the fine library founded by Archbishop Marsh, whatever the Latin and Greek writers had to say on the subject of gallantry. Here also it is probable that he made acquaintance with what the same preface calls "the graceful levity, the *grata protervitas* of a Rochester and a Sedley," and there probably he acquired that knowledge of Olympia Fulvia Morata, Alessandra Scala, and the other "Latin *blues*," which, long after, gave him the rare opportunity "to show off to Macaulay all such reading as *he* never read." Moore was always a surprising devourer of books, and his parents had profited by the presence of French émigrés to add a good knowledge of modern tongues to his store of classics; a fine memory completed his equipment for the academic side of literature.

Oddly enough, the desire for academic recognition seems to have prompted his first undertaking. Given a young man possessing a good supply of Greek and Latin, a large fund of miscellaneous knowledge, a strong taste for the amatory poets, and a remarkably neat turn with verse, it was natural enough that he should turn to translation of the classics. Anacreon, who had engaged his attention in schooldays, still held it: and about the time of his graduating, Moore went to the Provost of Trinity, Dr. Kearney, with a good handful of renderings from that poet, and suggested that his industry should be recognised by "some honour or reward." Dr. Kearney was sympathetic and flattering, but at the same time "expressed his doubts whether the Board could properly confer any public reward upon the translation of a work so amatory and convivial as the Odes of Anacreon." Nevertheless, he strongly advised publication, adding, with an agreeable touch of nature, "The young people will like it." It may be added that, when publication came to be arranged, Dr. Kearney was one of the only two subscribers found among "the monks of Trinity," as Moore contemptuously called them; and further, that he appears to have lent to the young poet his copy of Spaletti's edition—

one of two sent from the Pope to Trinity College by the intermediacy of the Catholic Archbishop Troy.

This, however, is to anticipate. It was in the spring of April 1799 that Mr. Thomas Moore set out to eat his first dinner at the Middle Temple. The proceeds of the little grocery business—of which Moore never was ashamed, and which never seems to have been a hindrance to him in society—were now to be sharply taxed. Mrs. Moore had long been hoarding against the journey to London, to gather the guineas which she now sewed up in the waistband of the adventurer's pantaloons. In some other part of the garments, "unknown to me" (Moore writes), "she had stitched in a scapular, a small piece of cloth blessed by the priest, which a fond superstition inclined her to believe would keep the wearer of it from harm." The journey was accomplished successfully, and quarters were found for the traveller at 44 George Street, Portman Square, by some Irish acquaintances. Except for his Irish connections, most of them people in a small way of life, apothecaries and the like, Moore was rather friendless in town. The custom of the Temple obliging each novice, as part of the form of initiation, to give a dinner to some brother Templars, embarrassed him at first, since he did not know a soul; and he was only relieved "by a young fellow, who, addressing me very politely, offered to collect for me the number of diners generally used on such occasions." It seems that he felt despondent, and a letter to his father suggests that he wrote querulously, asking leave to return home and give up the game. It is certain that he was immeasurably homesick, and each one of his letters to "my dearest father" and "my darling mother" teems with expressions of eagerness for the sight of them.

Nevertheless he was making his way, and, before a month was over, could write, "I need never be out of company if I chose it." He had formed also one of the two or three connections which dominated his life. Joseph Atkinson, secretary in Ireland to the Ordnance Board, who had made friends with the young singer in Dublin, gave him an introduction to Lord Moira (afterwards the second Marquis of Hastings). Moore, a few days after arriving, called on the great man, and was invited to dinner; the acquaintance must have progressed rapidly, for in the same year he was invited to pay a visit to Donington Park, Lord Moira's country seat, on his way back from spending the summer vacation in Ireland.

"This was of course at that time," Moore observes with that good-humoured candour which is a characteristic of him, "a great event in my life, and among the most vivid of my early English recollections is that of my first night at Donington, when Lord Moira, with that high courtesy for which he was remarkable, lighted me himself to my bedroom; and there was this stately personage stalking on before through the long lighted gallery, bearing in his hand my bed-candle which he delivered to me at the door of my apartment. I thought it all exceedingly fine and grand, but at the same time most uncomfortable, and little I foresaw how much at home and at my ease I should one day find myself in that great house."

After this visit, negotiations with a publisher for the issue of the *Anacreon*, which had been begun during Moore's first sojourn in London, were resumed, and probably the name of friendship with Lord Moira did no harm. At all events the business was conducted to a successful issue by Moore's friend, Dr. Hume; and on December 19, 1799, the new poet writes rapturously of getting a good number of names for the subscription, adding that he has "received two hard guineas already from Mr. Campbell and Mr. Tinker, which I hope will be lucky. They are the only guineas I ever kissed, and I have locked them up religiously." Dr. Lawrence, a scholar of repute, reported favourably of the translation. Mrs. Fitzherbert was added to the list of subscribers; and finally, to crown all, Moore wrote—

"My dear Mother, I have got the Prince's name and his permission that I should dedicate *Anacreon* to him. Hurra! Hurra!"

And before the translator returned to the home where he was so eagerly expected, he had been duly presented to "his Royal Highness, George Prince of Wales." "He is beyond doubt a man of very fascinating manners," the letter goes on (dated August 4, 1800); and indeed the Prince's remarks, as Moore reports them, were vastly civil:—

"The honour was entirely *his* in being allowed to put his name 'to a work of such merit.' He then said that he hoped when he returned to town in the winter, we should have many opportunities of *enjoying each other's society*; that he was passionately fond of music and had long heard of my talents in that way. Is not all this very fine?"

Very fine indeed. "But, my dearest mother, it has cost me a new coat. By-the-bye, I am still in my other tailor's debt." There one has in a nutshell the epitome of Moore's life, if the life were to be written from a hostile point of view. On the other hand, considered candidly, there is nothing more surprising than the small degree of harm done to Moore by his disproportionate success. For the son of a small Irish tradesman to find himself at the age of one-and-twenty flattered by the heir-apparent—at a time too when the heir-apparent was the all-conquering leader of society—was indeed a dazzling promotion. And from that day onwards, Moore never lost ground. He had through life his choice of whatever was most brilliant in social intercourse, and his choice showed a steadily growing sanity of judgment. Moreover, although his intimates were always people set on a pinnacle, he never for an instant wavered in his fidelity to the home where he had been brought up with so much love. The end of the letter which describes his introduction to the Prince deserves to be quoted for its natural warmth:—

> "Do not let any one read this letter but yourselves; none but a father and a mother can bear such egotising vanity; but I know who I am writing to—that they are interested in what is said of me, and that they are too partial not to tolerate my speaking of myself."

It is easy to see that Moore's success was mainly social at first rather than literary. Throughout life he exercised an irresistible charm. An infectious gaiety, joined to copious but never ill-natured wit, made his company desired by all; and his physical presence, though not striking, was always agreeable. Diminutive in size, and plain of feature, he gained something approaching beauty by the constant play of expression centred in his vivacious eyes and the mobile and beautiful mouth. More distinctive still, in youth at least, was his hair, which curled in long tendrils over his head. But the special charm which he exercised,—and it was doubtless of greater importance in youth, before his powers as a talker had matured—lay in a gift for singing, which appears to have been something peculiar to himself. He sang always to his own accompaniment, and the performance by all accounts approached declamation rather than ordinary song. Moore is the only poet of modern times who, like the ancient bards, lent to his own verses the added charm of musical expression. Poet first, musician afterwards, he gave the words for all they were worth, and he seems always to have counted it a failure, if there were no wet eyes among his hearers.

To this gift, nearer the actor's than either the musician's or the poet's, he owed probably the suddenness of his fame. It called attention to his literature; but the attention was well deserved, for this boyish production was notable, coming when it did.

In 1800, when the *Odes of Anacreon* appeared, Wordsworth and Coleridge had, it is true, published *Lyrical Ballads*. The revolution in taste had begun. Yet these fighters in the van beat heavily upon an armed opposition; and for the moment the tradition of Pope, as modified in different directions by Gray and Goldsmith, was passionately upheld against them. Burns, indeed, had already made a great breach in the solid academic phalanx, and had won through to acceptance. But newcomers, who preached such doctrines as were set out in the preface to *Lyrical Ballads*, roused fierce hostility; they came with their mouths full of arguments. Moore, on the other hand, troubled no man with controversy, yet was hardly more academic than they. Like them, he boldly discarded the eighteenth-century manner, still flourishing in the hands of Crabbe. "The early poets of our language," says the preface to Little's Poems, "were the models which Mr. Little selected for imitation." A glance at the *Anacreon* will show the truth of this observation. Take the third ode—

Listen to the Muse's lyre,
Master of the pencil's fire!
Sketch'd in painting's bold display,
Many a city first portray,
Many a city revelling free,
Warm with loose festivity.
Picture then a rosy train,
Bacchants straying o'er the plain,
Piping, as they roam along,
Roundelay or shepherd-song.
Paint me next, if painting may
Such a theme as this portray,
All the happy heaven of love
Which these blessed mortals prove.

Here the suggestion, if not of Fletcher's manner, at least of some manner contemporary with Fletcher, is unmistakable. But since the verses were put forward without comment, no one thought of objecting. It is like the fable of the Wind and the Sun: Moore's genial example relaxed the bonds of 'correctness' by far more quickly than Wordsworth's austere theorising.

The easy way is seldom so good as the hard way, and no one would put Moore's early work into comparison with the wonderful volume that was the fruit of the years spent by Wordsworth and Coleridge at Nether Stowey. Yet it is only just to emphasise the fact that Moore was the first to bring back to English that note of song, natural even in its artificiality, which is heard all through the sixteenth and seventeenth centuries, but, except by Blake, was never sounded during the eighteenth. One can readily imagine the delight with which a generation, nursed on Cowper and Crabbe, turned to these facile yet not vulgar harmonies. And the work, though seemingly so easy, was wrought with delicate care; Lord Moira noted, and Moore gratefully recorded the praise, that few among the best poets had been so strictly grammatical! Always a careful craftsman, Moore never worked harder than on this first attempt. But his labour detracted nothing from the flush of youth, the zest for enjoyment, which pervades the lines. 'The young people will like it,' probably in any generation, whenever they chance to read it.

Moore, however, could never reconcile himself to effacing altogether the traces of his study. *Lalla Rookh* testifies to his passion for footnotes, and the same unfortunate itch displays itself already in the *Anacreon*. We find him quoting, not only Ronsard and Lessing—a wide range for one-and-twenty—but commentators and authors by far more recondite—Cornelius de Pauw, the poetess Veronica Cambara, the Epistles of Alciphron, together with Aulus Gellius and Angerianus. One must remember, however, that Moore's age had a taste for what we should dismiss as pedantry—witness the polyglot jesting of Father Prout; and he doubtless obeyed a wise instinct when he opened his prefatory remarks in a manner worthy of the gentleman whom Dr. Primrose met in jail:—

> "There is but little known with certainty of the life of Anacreon. Chamæleon Heracleotes, who wrote upon the subject, has been lost in the general wreck of ancient literature."

In the next publication, which followed rapidly upon the success of the first, Moore dispensed with erudition. Censorious people shook their heads over the *Poetical Works of the late Thomas Little, Esq.*, and it must be allowed that the censure had some justification. In the remarks upon *Anacreon*, Moore had praised that poet because "his descriptions are warm; but the warmth is in the ideas not the words." There is certainly no grossness in the words of Mr. Thomas Little, but there is considerable warmth in his ideas—and indeed what could be more natural? Moore was an exceedingly healthy normal young man, strongly attracted towards the other sex, but exempt from any vehemences of passion. The tone of these lyrics is rather that of the Restoration poets than of the earlier Caroline school; there is prettiness, elegance, gaiety, rather than beauty; and, as in all his models, there is preoccupation rather with a sex than an individual. It is amatory poetry, not love-poetry; but in its own kind, it is as good as can be found. What could be better than

"Still the question I must parry,
Still a wayward truant prove,
Where I love I cannot marry,
Where I marry cannot love."

No other poet for a hundred years had got such elasticity and gaiety out of English rhythms as were to be found in these two early volumes. One need not claim high rank for this sort of poetry, but it would be ignorant to overlook the service which Moore was doing to all who after him came to handle English metre.

So much for his successes. The second volume is also interesting with records of his failures. The "Fragments of College Exercises" show a futile attempt to wield the heroic couplet with sonorous rhetoric. And in two other poems, *Reuben and Rose and The Ring*, we find Moore wandering off after the fashion of the German spectral ballad:—

"'Twas Reuben, but ah! he was deathly and cold,
And fleeted away like the spell of a dream."

And so on, with cold carcases and other properties of this form of composition, to which the poet never returned—wisely recognising that it was not for him to make readers' flesh creep.

In the meantime, while the *Anacreon* was passing into its second edition, and Little's Poems were making their appearance, Moore stayed in England, and his connection with Lord Moira grew closer. A great part of the year 1801 seems to have been spent by him at Donington, sometimes alone, when he worked hard in the library, shot rooks, repaired his complexion and slept sweetly, "not dreaming of ambition, though under the roof of an earl." In 1802 he had hopes of Lord Moira's coming into administration. But Lord Moira did not come in, and though considerable sums were earned by the Poems, Moore was obliged to borrow from his mother's brother. In the early part of 1803 a proposal was made to him, by Wickham, then Chief Secretary for Ireland, on behalf of the Irish Government. An Irish laureateship was to be established, with the same salary as the English, for the young Irish poet; the movers in this matter were Lord Moira and the always friendly Joe Atkinson. Our most definite record of the transaction is a letter from Moore to his mother, which makes it clear that he himself was prepared to accept the "paltry and degrading stipend," but was deterred by a letter from his father, which unfortunately we do not possess. The motive which he alleges was "the *urging* apprehension that my dears at home wanted it"; but since he was reassured that they stood in no instant necessity, he declined the offer. The letter however makes it perfectly clear that he looked forward at this time to a post provided by Government: legal studies in the meantime having lapsed.

These expectations were not wholly disappointed. In August Lord Moira's interest secured for him a place as registrar of a naval prize-court at Bermuda—an employment whose profits depended upon an active state of war in and about the West Indies.

The idea of so complete a separation from his home distressed him, and he tried to keep the facts from his mother as long as possible—discussing the project only by letters to his father and uncle. But on August 16th, John Moore—wrote to his son an admirable epistle (the only one from his pen that is preserved),—which deprecated the attempt to keep Mrs. Moore in the dark:—

"There could be no such deception carried on with her where you, or indeed any one of her family, were concerned, for she seems to know everything respecting them by instinct. It would not be doing her the justice she well deserves to exclude her from such confidence.... For my particular part, I think with you, that there is a singular chance, as well as a special interference of Providence, in your getting so honourable a situation at this very critical time.[1] I am sure no one living can possibly feel more sensibly than your poor mother and me do, at losing that comfort we so long enjoyed, of at least hearing from you once every week of your life that you were absent from us; for surely no parents had ever such happiness in a child; and much as we regret the wide separation which this situation of yours will for some time cause between us, we give you our full concurrence, and may the Almighty God spare and prosper you as you deserve."

Preparations went through quickly, and on September 22, 1803, Moore wrote, from Portsmouth, his "heart's farewell to the dear darlings at home." Carpenter, the publisher, had made advances which rendered departure possible, and so

"now all is smooth for my progress, and Hope sings in the shrouds of the ship that is to carry me. Good-by. God bless you all, dears of my heart."

[1] This was just after Emmet's rising.

CHAPTER II
EARLY MANHOOD AND MARRIAGE

The *Phaeton* frigate, on which Moore had procured a passage, left Spithead on September 25th, and on November 5th we find him writing to his mother from Norfolk in Virginia. The voyage, though rather rough, had been a pleasant experience, and, after his fashion, Moore had made friends with everybody on board. Thirty years later he was delighted with a passage in the *Naval Recollections* of Captain Scott, who had sailed as midshipman on the *Phaeton*. Scott's observation was, that he knew at that time nothing about Moore's poetry, but that the poet "appeared the life and soul of the company, and the loss of his fascinating society was frequently and loudly lamented by the officers long after he had quitted us in America." Moore was justifiably proud of having "left such an impression upon honest hearty unaffected fellows like those of the gun-room of the *Phaeton*," who would naturally—as he freely admits—have been prejudiced in the other sense. "I remember," he notes, "the first lieutenant saying to me after we had become intimate, 'I thought you the first day you came aboard, the damnedest conceited little fellow I ever saw, with your glass cocked up to your eye'; and then he mimicked the manner in which I made my first appearance." The first lieutenant's phrase is worth remembering as a frank piece of description.

Till the end of 1803 Moore was delayed in Virginia, waiting for a ship, and in the meanwhile writing long letters home full of the warmest affection, and of "longing for news of all his dears." In January he was lucky enough to get passage on another ship of war, the *Driver*, and reached Bermuda after seven days' sail in very heavy weather. His parting from Norfolk had been attended with the usual regrets; Mrs. Hamilton, wife of the British Consul, in whose home Moore had been most hospitably entertained, "cried, and said she never parted from any one so reluctantly," and her husband wrote him all possible letters of introduction.

Bermuda itself seemed, at the first view, a kind of fairyland, as he has recorded in the Epistle to Lady Donegal:—

"The morn was lovely, every wave was still,
When the first perfume of a cedar-hill
Sweetly awaked us, and, with smiling charms,
The fairy harbour woo'd us to its arms.
Gently we stole, before the languid wind,
Through plantain shades, that like an awning twined
And kiss'd on either side the wanton sails,
Breathing our welcome to these vernal vales;
While, far reflected o'er the wave serene,

Each wooded island shed so soft a green,
That the enamour'd keel, with whispering play,
Through liquid herbage seem'd to steal its way!
Never did weary bark more sweetly glide,
Or rest its anchor in a lovelier tide!
Along the margin, many a shining dome,
White as the palace of a Lapland gnome,
Brighten'd the wave;—in every myrtle grove
Secluded, bashful, like a shrine of love,
Some elfin mansion sparkled through the shade;
And, while the foliage interposing play'd,
Wreathing the structure into various grace,
Fancy would love, in glimpses vague, to trace
The flowery capital, the shaft, the porch,
And dream of temples, till her kindling torch
Lighted me back to all the glorious days
Of Attic genius; and I seem'd to gaze
On marble, from the rich Pentelic mount,
Gracing the umbrage of some Naiad's fount."

The letter which sketches his first impressions adds a touch of disenchantment, which Moore, remote always from realism, was careful to exclude from his verse:—

> "These little islands are thickly covered with cedar groves, through the vistas of which you catch a few pretty white houses, which my poetical short-sightedness always transforms into temples; and I often expect to see Nymphs and Graces come tripping from them, when I find, to my great disappointment, that a few miserable negroes is all 'the bloomy flush of life' it has to boast of."

What was more serious, the prospects of income also disenchanted him of his dream which was to make in Bermuda a home for himself and his family. So many prize-courts had been established, and so few causes were referred to his in Bermuda, that nothing but a Spanish war could hold out a prospect of large fees. Even that did not promise an income worth staying for, and Moore's decision was immediate—to finish the work he was engaged on for Carpenter, and then set out for home.

The precise nature of this engagement is not clear. He had from his first year in London been writing songs which were set to music by John Stevenson and others. In 1803 the poem from *Anacreon*, "Give me the Harp of Epic Song," had been arranged by Stevenson as a glee, and its performance by the Irish Harmonic Club so pleased Lord Hardwicke, then Viceroy, that he conferred a knighthood on the composer. Moore's last letter on leaving England contained directions for collecting his songs to be published together, and the letters from Bermuda made constant reference to this project, which, however, was never executed. In the meantime, as his work testifies, he was busy writing verses; even aboard ship, he had not been idle. And, as usual, his verse writing was largely amatory. Later in life, he records with some amusement that a lady in Bermuda was pointed out as the original "Nea" to whom several poems are addressed, and he wonders if they had hit on the right person, adding that there were at least *two* who had a claim.

Festivities, as a matter of course, surrounded him, and he was happy as a king, but for one lack. Up till March 19th, no letter had reached him from Ireland.

> "Oh darling mother," he cries, "six months now and I know as little of *home* as of things most remote from my heart and recollection.... The signal post which announces when any vessels are in sight of the island is directly before my window, and often do I look to it with a heart sick 'from hope deferred.'"

In the end of April he left his post, having, in an evil hour, appointed a deputy to discharge its duties and share the profits. The *Boston* frigate took him to New York, and its captain, John Douglas, afterwards admiral, formed a friendship with the poet of which proofs were given again and again. In 1811, he met Moore in London, after five years had passed without a word or a letter exchanged. Douglas had just come into a legacy of ten thousand pounds, and was going to sea with seven hundred pounds standing to his name in Coutts's.

> "Now, my dear little fellow," he said, "here is a blank check, which you may fill up while I am away, for as much of that as you may want."

Moore, who declined the offer, as he declined many others of like nature, might well comment on a man's "bringing back the warmth of friendship so unchilled after an absence of five years." Nor was that the end of it. In 1814 Douglas, then Admiral on the Jamaica Station, offered Moore the Secretaryship, "in case of war a sure fortune," with a house and land to be at the poet's disposal; and, as Moore notes, the offer was not only friendly but courageous, for Douglas owed his appointment to Court interest, and at that moment the Whig satirist was in the worst odour with the Regent and all his surroundings.

The immediate boon, gladly accepted, of the passage from Bermuda to America, and thence to England, was the more important, as it enabled

Moore to devote the money, which had been set aside for his passage, to seeing the New World. He sailed from New York to Norfolk, and thence set out for Baltimore; and the journey in American stage coaches appears to have shaken out of him whatever remained of his early illusions about the "land of the free." America at that time was beyond dispute inchoate, amorphous, and ugly in all senses, and Moore's instincts were anything but democratic. At Philadelphia, "the only place in America which can boast of any literary society," he found his writings well known, and met with a flattering reception, which pleased him; a Mrs. Hopkinson in particular showed him attentions which elicited the poem, "Alone by the Schuylkill a wanderer roved." Returning to New York, he found that the *Boston* must go to Halifax, and could not sail before August. This offered an opportunity of journeying to Canada overland, and accordingly he sailed up the Hudson River, through "the most bewildering succession of romantic objects that I could ever have conceived." The Oneida Indians charmed him by their courtesy, the rivers and virgin forests wrought upon his sensibilities, and when he came within hearing of the roar of Niagara, it seemed to him dreadful that "any heart born for sublimities should be doomed to breathe away its hours amidst the miniature productions of this world without seeing what shapes Nature can assume, what wonders God *can* give birth to."

The sight, not so much of the falls as of "the mighty flow descending with calm magnificence" towards them, moved him passionately; and the journey, "seventeen hundred miles of rattling and tossing, through woods, lakes, rivers, etc.," did him good. He reached Quebec much gratified by many kindnesses. The captain of the vessel which carried him across Lake Ontario refused to take money from the poet, and a poor watchmaker at Niagara insisted that a job done should be accepted "as the only mark of respect he could pay to one he had heard so much of but never expected to meet with." At Halifax more proofs of what, later in life, he called, with great justice, his "friendly fame," greeted him, in the shape of courtesies from the Governors of Lower Canada and of Nova Scotia. It is Moore's great distinction that he gave real pleasure to all sorts and conditions of men; and they showed it by treating him as if he had conferred obligations on them. The feeling which is to-day so widespread among his countrymen animated in his lifetime all the English-speaking world. Yet it is surprising to read such instances of widespread celebrity when we remember that at this time he was the author only of translations from a pseudo-classic, and of a small volume of verses, not explicitly acknowledged, and by no means wholly decorous.

His American experiences ended about a year after he left Europe, and on November 12, 1804, he dated his letter rapturously "Plymouth, Old England once more." "Oh dear," he goes on, "to think that in ten days I may see a letter from home, written but a day or two before, warm from your hands, and with your very breath almost upon it, instead of lingering out month after month without a gleam of intelligence, without anything but dreams."

Nevertheless, a good many months elapsed before the returned exile could make his way home. London held out open arms to him; the Prince was very friendly; "every one I ever knew in this big city seems delighted to see me back in it." And so, although in January 1805 he was hoping that six weeks would see the end of his labours on the forthcoming volume that was to clear off all obligations, August found him still urging the necessity of finishing his work without any avoidable delay. It seems that he went home to Dublin in the autumn, and Lord Moira, then Commander-in-Chief in Scotland, wrote a letter accepting the dedication of the forthcoming *Epistles and Odes*, in the most honorific language.

The next year, 1806, saw the formation of the Ministry of "All the Talents," and for a moment it seemed as if Moira would be included. His protégé's hopes ran high, but they were dashed. A small appointment was offered to Moore, but refused by him on the ground that it would be "better to wait till something worthier both of his generosity and my ambition should occur"; and at the same time the young man suggested that it would be a simpler matter to find an appointment for his father, and that such a favour would earn even more gratitude. Lord Moira at once acted on the suggestion, and John Moore was appointed to a barrack-mastership in Dublin. But Moore by no means relinquished hopes of the Irish commissionership which still dangled before his eyes, and the letters to his most intimate friends of this period, Lady Donegal and her sister, Miss Godfrey, abound with references to his expectations. Nevertheless, he had fully made up his mind, once the new poems were fairly launched, to return to Ireland and leave his interests in Lord Moira's care, when an unforeseen event led to one of the best-known passages in his life.

It arose from the publication in 1806 of the new volume, *Epistles, Odes, and other Poems.* Carpenter evidently laid out money on the production of this quarto, with its frontispiece representing the *Phaeton* under sail off the peak of the Azores; and his expectations were not disappointed. The Epistles contained in the volume, nine in number, were impressions of travel on shipboard and on land; the best is certainly that to Lady Donegal (already quoted), which describes the arrival at Bermuda; and perhaps the best known is that to Atkinson, from which a few lines may be given:—

"'Twas thus, by the shade of the Calabash Tree,
With a few, who could feel and remember like me,
The charm, that to sweeten my goblet I threw,
Was a tear to the past and a blessing on you!

"Oh! say, do you thus, in the luminous hour
Of wine and of wit, when the heart is in flower,
And shoots from the lip, under Bacchus's dew,
In blossoms of thought ever springing and new—
Do you sometimes remember, and hallow the brim
Of your cup with a sigh, as you crown it to him
Who is lonely and sad in these valleys so fair,
And would pine in elysium, if friends were not there?"

More immediate notice than was bestowed on these passages of mingled description and sentiment fell to the three epistles in which Moore for the first time tried his hand at satire,—moved to it by the corruptions of the young Republic, where he found

"All youth's transgression with all age's chill
The apathy of wrong, the bosom's ice,
A slow and cold stagnation into vice."

These experiments in satire of the accepted type, written in Pope's metre, have, however, no more permanent value than the two odes, equally academic—one upon the "Fall of Hebe" and one described as a "Fragment of a Mythological Hymn to Love." It is safe to say that the book owed its very wide popularity to the songs and shorter lyrics. Two of the songs had an immense vogue—"The Woodpecker" and the still popular "Canadian Boat-song" ("Faintly as tolls the evening chime"), written to an air suggested to Moore by the chant of his oarsmen as he travelled down the St. Lawrence.

In addition to these were a number of amatory verses, some of them at least as well calculated to scandalise as anything in the posthumous works of Mr. Little. It is true that, read to-day, these do not seem to call for any extreme censure. They are glorifications expressly of fugitive loves, dwelling rather on pleasure than on passion, and one might argue whether they were the more or the less dangerous on that account. But there is no doubt that Moore maintained the reputation which he had earned for licentious poetry. Those who wished to rebuke Byron's first indiscretions called him "a young Moore." It is, therefore, not to be wondered at that the *Edinburgh Review*, in its character of *censor morum*, having passed over the *Anacreon* and Little's Poems, should come heavily down upon this renewed offence—describing Moore as "the most licentious of modern versifiers, and the most poetical of those who in our time have devoted their talents to the propagation of immorality." But the second paragraph of the article went beyond fair bounds when it attributed to Moore "a cold-blooded attempt to corrupt the purity of unknown and unsuspecting readers." Jeffrey had a right to say that the poet blended mere sensuality with the language "of exalted feeling and tender emotion"; but no critic can endorse the offensive passage in which he describes Moore as "stimulating his jaded fancy for new images of impurity." The best apology for whatever in the book needs excuse, is that Moore gave in his verse too ready an outlet to the ordinary exuberances of a pleasure-loving young man's temperament, and that he seldom pretended to conceal the transitory nature of his feelings.

And, in the sequel, Jeffrey admitted in writing that he had been too severe. A good deal, however, had happened first. Moore's first impulse does not seem to have been belligerent, and as the purpose of calling Jeffrey out dawned on him, there dawned also a difficulty. Jeffrey was probably in Scotland (a letter from Moore to George Thomson, editor of *Select Scottish Airs*, etc., contains an inquiry as to his whereabouts), and this seemed to involve a journey to Edinburgh for which "the actual but too customary state of my finances" (Moore writes in the memoir of this transaction) "seriously disabled me." But, on coming to London, he learnt from Rogers that Jeffrey was also in town, and on ascertaining the fact, immediately went to look for a second. The friend to whom he first addressed himself having counselled delay, the affair was entrusted to Dr. Hume, and a cartel was written in such terms that there could be only one answer. Jeffrey referred Hume to Horner, and a meeting was fixed for the next morning at Chalk Farm. But neither combatant possessed pistols, and it was left for Moore to borrow them from a friend. Moreover, on reaching the ground, Hume found that Jeffrey's second knew nothing of firearms, and the task of loading both pistols was entrusted to him; while in the meantime the two principals, left together, walked up and down, conversing very agreeably. Presently the seconds returned and placed their men; but, as the pistols were raised, police officers jumped from an ambush. The lender of the pistols had been indiscreet and revealed the secret over-night at Lord Fincastle's dinner-table; Lord Fincastle had immediately communicated with Bow Street, with the result that early next morning the poet and his critic found themselves in durance till bail was given.

So far, nothing very remarkable had happened. But Moore, after going away, remembered that he had left the pistols behind, and returned to get them. The officer, however, refused to give them up, and made the disagreeable explanation that foul play was suspected; a bullet having been found in Moore's pistol, but none in that taken from Jeffrey. To make matters worse, a report in the newspapers substituted the word "pellet" for "bullet," and pleasantries were rife about author and critic fighting with pellets of paper. Moore was furious, and persuaded Horner to draw up an account of the matter, to be signed by the two seconds, but Hume "took fright at the ridicule brought upon us by the transaction" and refused to have any more to do with it. More than thirty years elapsed before Moore was reconciled to the friend who thus failed him, and his wrath was not unreasonable, since the explanation published by himself in the *Times* naturally carried little weight. Yet it afterwards gave him ground for challenging Byron. Thus closely connected are Moore's two attempts at duelling; and there is nothing more characteristic of his life than the fact that in each case his challenge was only the introduction to a friendship of the sincerest and most honourable kind.

After the close of this episode Moore returned to Dublin,—some hackwork for Carpenter on Sallust defraying his expenses—and remained there till the spring of 1807, reading daily in Marsh's library for about three hours and a half. "I have written nothing since I came here," he tells Miss Godfrey— dating his letter Dublin, February 23rd—"except one song which everybody says is the best I have ever composed." The exception is notable, for this song may have been one of the first of the *Irish Melodies*.

The inception of Moore's most famous work was due to a publisher's suggestion. In 1797 (or perhaps a year earlier), Bunting's collection of Irish Airs had been issued, and Moore tells us that his interest in them was encouraged by his friend Edward Hudson. Even before his departure for Bermuda the young Irish poet had shown his skill in fitting words for singing; and songs by him had been issued by Carpenter, by Rhames of Dublin, and by other firms. When he returned home after an absence which extended from the summer of 1803 to the autumn of 1806, he returned with fame greatly augmented by his latest volume, and presumably the vogue of his singing was not less in Dublin than elsewhere. What the song was that he refers to in his letter to Miss Godfrey, we do not know; but it is exceedingly likely to have been the lines on Emmet, which occupied a prominent place in the first number of the *Melodies*. One can very well believe that the fame of some song by Moore on an Irish theme may have suggested to William Power, owner of a music warehouse in Dublin, the proposal which he made—namely, that Moore should collaborate with Sir John Stevenson in producing a series of Irish Melodies.

The following prefatory letter, addressed by Moore to Stevenson, was issued by the publisher in his preliminary announcement to the first and second numbers:—

> "I feel very anxious that a work of this kind should be undertaken. We have too long neglected the only talent for which our English neighbours ever deigned to allow us any credit. Our National Music has never been properly collected; and while the composers of the Continent have enriched their Operas and Sonatas with Melodies borrowed from Ireland—very often without even the honesty of acknowledgment—we have left these treasures, in a great

degree, unclaimed and fugitive. Thus our Airs, like too many of our countrymen, have, for want of protection at home, passed into the service of foreigners. But we are come, I hope, to a better period of both Politics and Music; and how much they are connected, in Ireland at least, appears too plainly in the tone of sorrow and depression which characterizes most of our early Songs.

"The task which you propose to me, of adapting words to these airs, is by no means easy. The Poet, who would follow the various sentiments which they express, must feel and understand that rapid fluctuation of spirits, that unaccountable mixture of gloom and levity, which composes the character of my countrymen, and has deeply tinged their Music. Even in their liveliest strains we find some melancholy note intrude—some minor Third or flat Seventh—which throws its shade as it passes, and makes even mirth interesting. If Burns had been an Irishman (and I would willingly give up all our claims upon Ossian for him), his heart would have been proud of such music, and his genius would have made it immortal.

"Another difficulty (which is, however, purely mechanical) arises from the irregular structure of many of those airs, and the lawless kind of metre which it will in consequence be necessary to adapt to them. In these instances, the Poet must write, not to the eye, but to the ear; and must be content to have his verses of that description which Cicero mentions, *'Quos si cantu spoliaveris nuda remanebit oratio.'* That beautiful Air, 'The Twisting of the Rope,' which has all the romantic character of the Swiss *Ranz des Vaches*, is one of those wild and sentimental rakes which it will not be very easy to tie down in sober wedlock with Poetry. However, notwithstanding all these difficulties, and the very moderate portion of talent which I can bring to surmount them, the design appears to me so truly National, that I shall feel much pleasure in giving it all the assistance in my power."

Leicestershire, *Feb.* 1807.

The date is curious. Moore, writing to Miss Godfrey on February 23rd from Dublin, made no mention of this project. He certainly crossed in the end of February, and took up his abode (as was now his recognised privilege) in solitary state at Donington. From there he wrote to his mother for a copy of Bunting's *Airs*, and also of Miss Owenson's—to be got from Power. In April he sends her "an inclosure for Power" to be forwarded immediately—and this was probably the prefatory letter. For Mr. Andrew Gibson's researches have discovered in the *Belfast Commercial Chronicle* of May 28, 1807, a paragraph relating to Power's projected "Collection of the best Original Irish Melodies," which concludes by citing a portion of Moore's prefatory letter, and the date affixed is "Leicestershire, *April* 1807."

For what reason the month should be given as February in all published editions of the *Melodies*, it is hard to conceive. But the result has been a widespread bibliographical error, since the publication is always assigned to 1807. Mr. Gibson, however, has unearthed various announcements in the *Freeman's Journal*, of which two speak in October of the work as "shortly to be published," and another, on April 8th, 1808, as "just published." The latter advertisement invited subscribers for "the succeeding numbers"; names were to be given to the publisher, William Power, in Dublin, or in London to his brother James Power, who had recently established a similar place of business in the Strand.

Under the original scheme, Moore was only to have been one of "several distinguished Literary Characters" from whom "Power has had promises of assistance." But his success precluded all competition. The twenty-four songs comprised in the first two numbers include some of his very best and much of his most popular work, and it is interesting to note that almost the whole of them must have been written in Ireland. His stay at Donington lasted till June, and during the earlier part of it he was certainly engaged on poetry. But except for an excursion to Tunbridge, to visit Lady Donegal and her sister, he went nowhere else in England, and he was back in Dublin by the end of August. In the remaining months of that summer he paid the visit to the Vale of Ovoca which gave occasion to his lyric, "The Meeting of the Waters." A footnote to the first edition of the first number explains that—

> "'The Meeting of the Waters' forms a part of that beautiful scenery which lies between Rathdrum and Arklow in the County of Wicklow, and these lines were suggested to me by a visit to this romantic spot in the summer of the present year (1807)."

It appears also, from a letter to Miss Godfrey, that in May 1807 his solitude at Donington was interrupted by the advent of a large house-party, and one may fairly say that, except for what he may have done in the space of about three months, the whole of the lyrics of the first two numbers were composed in the country where the airs themselves had their origin.

Moreover, during his stay at Donington, other work than the *Melodies* engaged him. He tells Lady Donegal, "to God's pleasure and both our comforts," that he is not writing love verses.

"I begin at last to find out that *politics* is the only thing minded in this country, and that it is better even to rebel against government than to have nothing to do with it; so I am writing politics."

The result of this determination was seen in the publication which appeared towards the end of 1808—*Corruption and Intolerance*, two more satirical essays in the Popian manner. These productions were issued by Carpenter in a thin octavo, eked out with a vast deal of notes. Moore had not yet arrived at his characteristic manner of expression in satire, and neither poem deserves much notice. Yet there was talent and to spare in lines like these:—

"Hence the rich oil, that from the Treasury steals,
Drips smooth o'er all the Constitution's wheels,
Giving the old machine such pliant play,
That Court and Commons jog one joltless way,
While Wisdom trembles for the crazy car,
So gilt, so rotten, carrying fools so far."

And at the close of the poem there is a note of unaccustomed fierceness in the reference to Castlereagh:

"See yon smooth lord, whom nature's plastic pains
Would seem to've fashion'd for those Eastern reigns
When eunuchs flourish'd, and such nerveless things
As men rejected were the chosen of Kings."

The lines on Intolerance were described as fragmentary—"the imperfect beginning of a long series of Essays upon the same important subject"; and the political attitude of the whole was sufficiently described on the title-page, where the lines were described as "Addressed to an Englishman by an Irishman."

Moore disclaimed in the preface any attachment to either English party, and the publication was, at least formally, anonymous. Yet we find him admitting that he had projected a journey to London to arrange for the republication of these poems, reinforced by others in the same kind, "in the hope that I *might* catch the eye of some of our patriotic politicians, and thus be enabled to serve both *myself* and the *principles* which I cherish." Carpenter, however, threw cold water on the scheme, and the rebuff touched the poet's susceptibilities so sharply, that he determined not to trust himself again in London "without the means of commanding a supply." For this, his past successes were no resource, since it was always Moore's imprudent habit to sell work outright. Little's Poems were being constantly reprinted, with no benefit to their author; and as for the songs, he writes in August 1808, "I

- 29 -

quite threw away the Melodies. They will make that little, smooth fellow's fortune."

In 1809 another thin octavo, called *The Sceptic*, and signed by "The Author of Corruption and Intolerance," was issued by Carpenter: Rogers (who from this period onward ranks high among Moore's advisers) protesting against his continuance with this publisher. But the book attracted little notice; and the lack of success which attended these attempts in serious satire very naturally turned Moore back into the work where his triumph had been most gratifying. In January 1810 he published, with a dedication to Lady Donegal, the third instalment of his *Irish Melodies*, and it bears the stamp of its birthplace. The political passion is by far more openly declared than before, and in two or three of the lyrics—notably "After the Battle" and "The Irish Peasant to his Mistress"—it attains as high a pitch of poetry as is reached anywhere in its author's work. Part of the former may be quoted, if only to show the similarity between its motive and the central idea of "The Fire Worshippers."

"Night closed around the conqueror's way,
And lightnings showed the distant hill,
Where those who lost that dreadful day
Stood few and faint, but fearless still!
The soldier's hope, the patriot's zeal,
For ever dimmed, for ever crossed—
Oh! who shall say what heroes feel,
When all but life and honour's lost?

"The last sad hour of freedom's dream,
And valour's task, moved slowly by,
While mute they watched till morning's beam
Should rise and give them light to die."

The twelve lyrics of this number, together with the thin brochure of *The Sceptic*, are all that Moore had to show for the months from July or August 1808 to December 1810, which make up the only long continuous period of his adult life spent in Ireland. We have little record of his doings during that time, and the most significant part of it is to be found in a little quarto, privately printed, which details the performances of the Kilkenny Theatre. Published in 1825, this little book was made the subject by Moore of an article in the *Edinburgh Review* for October 1827. Its preface sketches briefly the history of a craze for private theatricals which pervaded Ireland in the years from 1760 onwards. But nowhere else does the passion appear to have established itself so strongly as on the banks of the Nore, where a company was got together in 1802 under the auspices of a local gentleman, Mr. Richard Power. Originally the performances lasted for a week, but soon the programme was arranged for a fortnight, and in one case for three weeks. The event was annual till 1819, when the Kilkenny Theatre was closed for ever—marking, as Moore says in his review, the end of the social period in Ireland.

Moore, as we have seen, returned to Ireland in August 1808, and on the 10th of October following he made his *début* at Kilkenny; not alone, for Mr. Power in that year obtained two notable recruits. Isaac Corry, one of Moore's most lasting and agreeable friends, joined the troupe, and remained faithful for years; moreover, the genial Joe Atkinson, who, we may guess, introduced these new actors, wrote the prologue. Moore was only at this time a tentative member of the company, and played three days out of the twelve. We find the *Leinster Journal* (whose exceedingly well-written notices of the performances are regularly quoted in the volume) noting, to begin with, that "the Theatrical Company have been favoured with the presence of Anacreon Moore." But on the 22nd October the new recruit made his first appearance in the small part of David in *The Rivals*, and "kept the audience in a roar by his Yorkshire dialect and rustic simplicity." The success was renewed by him as Mungo in *The Padlock*, and as Spado (a singing part) in *A Castle of Andalusia*. Next year a list of plays that ran from the 2nd to the 21st of October was produced, and we read that "the delight and darling of the Kilkenny audience appears to be Anacreon Moore," who wrote the prologue for the occasion, and "spoke it in his own bewitching manner." "The vivacity and *naïveté* of his manner, the ease and archness of his humour, and the natural sweetness of his voice have quite enamoured us." In the solid Shaksperian part of the programme—for Mr. Power and his men did not shrink before *Macbeth* and *Othello*—this actor took no part. What he did play in was the farce *Peeping Tom of Coventry*—and, let it be carefully observed, the Lady Godiva was Miss E. Dyke. Miss E. Dyke was a beautiful girl, then aged fourteen; her sister, Miss H. Dyke, had appeared the year before, and both, it seems, were professional actresses. Of their talents the recorder in the *Leinster Journal* makes no mention, but he is eloquent again and again on the successes of Mr. Moore, and the performances of 1809 appear to have marked an epoch. In 1810 Moore was again (and for the last time) a performer. The critic inclines to cavil at the slightness of the part given to this favourite, and emphasises Moore's cleverness with enthusiasm. But, indeed, on two of the evenings Moore had the stage entirely to himself, when, between the plays, he sat down to a piano and spoke his *Melologue upon National Music*, verses which he had written to be declaimed by Miss Smith at the Dublin Theatre for a benefit night, and which were afterwards published in pamphlet form.

All this pleasant gaiety had two consequences, of which the less important may be first noted. In January 1809, three months after Moore's first appearance at Kilkenny, Rogers writes: "I am delighted with your intention to make your debut on the stage—as an author I mean. Of your fame as an actor, I have had many reverberations." Nothing more came of the intention at the moment, but in December 1810 Moore returned to London after a two years' absence, and writes of many visits "from booksellers, musicsellers, managers, etc., with offers for books, songs, and plays. I rather think," he adds, "I may give something to Covent Garden." The result was that sometime in the following summer he was trembling upon a manager's verdict, and on September 4th, 1811, saw with no pleasurable feelings, the production of his opera, *M.P. or The Blue Stocking*, at the English Opera House. The piece was a failure, despite a friendly press; and the songs from it, all that Moore cared to preserve, are by no means good examples of his work. For many years afterwards the stage tempted him, as a means of earning money, but he never returned to the charge.

The other sequel of the Kilkenny theatricals was of very different character. In the end of 1808 Rogers, answering a letter, remarks, "Your sketch of Ireland is most gloomy." Twelve months later, and after Miss E. Dyke's first appearance in Mr. Power's company, Rogers writes, "I am rejoiced to think you are happy, which indeed you cannot fail to be while you are making others so; but don't let the Graces supplant the Muses." It is hardly rash to infer that Moore had written a cheerful account of the 1809 festival at Kilkenny. October 1810 saw the last appearance in the Kilkenny bills of Mr. Moore and Miss E. Dyke. Early in December Moore ran back to London to interview "booksellers, musicsellers, managers, etc." In January he returned to Dublin for a few weeks. February saw him in town again; and in March it appears that he has "at last got a little bedroom about two miles from town where I shall try now and then for a morning's work." On March 25th he was married to Miss Dyke at St. Martin's Church; but the marriage was kept a secret from his parents till the month of May following.

On the face of it, nothing could have seemed less promising than this alliance. Moore had to live by his wits; he was now in his thirty-second year, he had lived with people of expensive habits and, in a sense, lived fast. Allowing for some rhetoric, one may take as a fair account the description of his feelings which he wrote to Lady Donegal in the summer preceding the last bout of theatricals at Kilkenny—when, presumably, his fate was settled.

> "I wish," he says, "I could give you even a tolerable account of what I have done; but I don't know how it is, both my mind and heart appear to have lain for some time completely fallow, and even the usual crop of *wild oats* has not been forthcoming. What is the reason of this? I believe there is in every man's life (at least in every man who has lived as if he knew how to live) one blank interval, which takes place at that period when the gay desires of youth are

just gone off, and he has not yet made up his mind as to the feelings or pursuits that succeed them—when the last blossom has fallen away, and yet the fruit continues to look harsh and unpromising—a kind of *interregnum* which takes place upon the demise of love, before ambition and worldliness have seated themselves upon the vacant throne."

One can easily imagine a gentleman who writes in this strain making, some few months later, a match with a penniless and beautiful girl of sixteen, whose situation had so little to recommend it that he kept the whole affair dark even from his parents. It would not have been so likely a guess that he would make her the most affectionate of husbands, or that she would turn out to be the most helpful of wives. There are few things more significant in a man's history than his choice of a consort, and stress must be laid on this marriage. In the first place, it should be remarked that Moore, with an equipment for the business which might have made any fortune-hunter envious, never showed the least inclination to marry for money. Secondly, although himself among the most brilliant of talkers, finding his chief enjoyment in such talk as was heard, for instance, at Holland House, he married a girl who probably had little education and certainly possessed only the intelligence of the heart. He married, doubtless, for beauty; but probably not without discerning that this girl of sixteen had qualities of prudence, order, and courage which amply justified his choice. She must have possessed also a great charm, for the most difficult to please among Moore's friends were immediately subjugated. Rogers, who had a sincere and lifelong affection for the young poet, took her from the first into his good graces, and his letters all contain some pleasant word of remembrance to Psyche, as he christened her. In a later day, Psyche and her babies were the guests of that rigidly celibate old bachelor, and did not lack invitation to return. Miss Godfrey, another shrewd and loyal well-wisher, wrote six months after the marriage:—

> "Be very sure, my dear Moore, that if you have got an amiable, sensible wife, extremely attached to you, as I am certain you have, it is only in the long run of life that you can know the full value of the treasure you possess. If you did but see, as I see with bitter regret in a very near connection of my own, the miserable effects of marrying a vain fool devoted to fashion, you would bless your stars night and day for your good fortune, and, to say the truth, you were as likely a gentleman to get into a scrape that way as any that I know. You were always the slave of beauty, say

what you please; it covered a multitude of sins in your eyes, and I never can cease wondering at your good luck after all is said and done."

Certainly, Bessy Moore was as little of the "vain fool devoted to fashion" as could be found. The two lived together, in Bury Street, for a year, till after the birth of their first child,—Barbara—born in February 1812. Soon after this, a parliamentary crisis raised Moore's hopes of Lord Moira's advancement, and his own depending on it, to fever height. They were soon dashed. Lord Moira was a staunch supporter of the Catholic claims, and the ministry had decided to do nothing for the Catholics. For the moment at least Moore took the defeat as final and wrote with some bitterness to Lady Donegal:—

> "In Lord Moira's exclusion from all chances of power, I see an end to the long hope of my life; and my intention is to go far away into the country, there to devote the remainder of my life to the dear circle I am forming around me, to the quiet pursuit of literature, and, I hope, of goodness."

Whatever spleen is to be traced in this letter soon vanished. On March 6, a letter to Miss Godfrey marks Moore's definitive breaking with his old habit of precarious reliance upon the prospect of patronage. Literary earnings, which he had hitherto regarded as a mere temporary means of meeting embarrassments, were now to become the sole support of himself and his family; and he bids good-bye with a cheerful courage to "all the hope and suspense in which the prospect of Lord Moira's advancement" had kept him for so many years.

> "It has been a sort of *Will o' the Wisp* to me all my life, and the only thing I regret is, that it was not extinguished sooner, for it has led me a sad dance."

Retirement from town was necessary, for the general curiosity "to see Moore's wife" threatened to become ruinous; and one may be very sure that if Bessy refused invitations "to the three most splendid assemblies in town," it was her doing and not her husband's. In the choice of a neighbourhood, access to a library had to be considered, and Moore naturally enough looked for a home near Donington Park. It was accordingly at Kegworth, a few miles from Lord Moira's seat, that he installed himself; but the proximity was unfortunate, for the cabinet crisis continued, and the Prince Regent's personal reliance on Lord Moira sustained Moore's hopes. In the autumn came news that Moira was to be Governor-General of India, and Moore's friends immediately settled it that the poet would accompany him as secretary. The remaining months of 1812 were embittered by hope deferred, which some expressions let fall by Lord Moira helped to quicken. But the great man and his household came and went, making it clear to Moore that he could count on nothing but continued good-will. The suggestion of an exchange of patronage made by Lord Moira was fortunately put aside; Moore replying that he would "rather struggle on as he was than take anything that would have the effect of tying up his tongue under such a system as the present."

Thus, in January 1813, with Moira's departure for India, the long relation between the patron and client ended, not without mutual embarrassment. Yet Moore was grateful for the kindly attentions heaped upon himself and his Bessy, who was then in a state to need them. Her second confinement, again of a daughter, Olivia, took place in March; and, as soon as she could be moved, Moore and she accepted willingly the invitation of a cordial friend, one Mrs. Ready, and settled into her house, Oakhanger Hall, for the summer. It had been decided to give up the Kegworth cottage, and look out for some pleasanter home; and a plan had also been arranged which made Moore glad to leave his wife in friendly company during the months of the London season.

In 1811, a fourth number of the *Irish Melodies* had been published, and Moore's cumulative success as a song-writer had tempted the brothers Power to make an offer which ensured to him and his at least a livelihood for the term of the agreement. They were to pay £500 a year for the monopoly of Moore's musical compositions.[1] The arrangement thus entered into lasted for over twenty years, and was financially Moore's backbone. But both Moore himself and the Powers recognised that the vogue of these songs was largely due to Moore's own singing of them, and it was consequently settled at Kegworth, that the singer should go up to town alone for the month of May. Bessy was naturally reluctant at first; "indeed," Moore wrote to Power, "it was only on my representing to her that my songs would all remain a dead letter with you, if I did not go up in the gay time of the year, and give them life by singing them about, that she agreed to my leaving her." The practice, once fixed, became habitual. For the next thirty years Moore was never long enough absent from town to lose touch with the society which never ceased to welcome him; while Bessy remained at home, minding the babies and keeping down the bills. Few women, even without her beauty, would have consented to the situation; but she accepted it cheerfully, and regretted only the absences of her husband. She had her reward. Lord John Russell writes in his introduction, concerning Moore's regard for his wife:—

> "From 1811, the year of his marriage, to 1852, that of his death, this excellent and beautiful person received from him the homage of a lover enhanced by all the gratitude, all the confidence, which the daily and hourly happiness he enjoyed were sure to inspire. Thus, whatever amusement he

might find in society, whatever literary resources he might seek elsewhere, he always returned to his home with a fresh feeling of delight. The time he had been absent had been a time of exertion and exile; his return restored him to tranquillity and to peace. Keen as was his natural sense of enjoyment, he never balanced between pleasure and happiness. His letters and his journal bear abundant trace of these natural and deep-seated affections."

It is, indeed, true that few men of whom one reads appear to have got more pleasure out of their home than Moore, and the first home where he really settled down to quiet domesticity was at Mayfield Cottage, "near the pretty town of Ashbourne," "a little nutshell of a thing, yet with a room to spare for a friend." The early letters abound in descriptive touches, one of which shows Bessy busy superintending workmen, while the head of the family and his little Barbara rolled in the hay outside. The neighbourhood, too, was full of welcome and small gaieties. Bessy appeared at a local ball and excited a great sensation by her beauty.

"She wore a turban that night to please me, and she looks better in it than anything else; for it strikes almost everybody that sees her, how like the form and expression of her face are to Catalani's, and a turban is the thing for that sort of character."

It is as well to remember that this prudent little dame was then aged eighteen—in spite of her two babies; and Moore, though getting up in years by comparison, was youthful enough in spirits.

"You would have laughed to see Bessy and me going to dinner," he writes to his mother. "We found in the middle of our walk, that we were near half an hour too early, so we set to practising country dances in the middle of a retired green lane, till the time was expired."

[1] From this, however, deduction was made for part of the payments to Sir John Stevenson, and afterwards to Henry Bishop. Moore's method (if it could be called a method) was to draw on Power for what he wanted; and these deductions amounted to much more than he supposed. The natural result was a quarrel when in the long run accounts were made up.

CHAPTER III
LALLA ROOKH

There was scarcely a period in Moore's life when prospects looked brighter for him than just after his settlement at Mayfield Cottage. He had clearly decided on living in seclusion till he should have finished the important work on which he had been engaged already, off and on, during a full year. In the summer of 1812, enough of *Lalla Rookh* existed to be shown to Rogers, when he and Moore took a tour together through the Peak country; and Rogers's criticism left the poet rather out of conceit with his work. Next year found him again dispirited, for the *Giaour* had appeared, and Moore writes:—

> "Never was anything more unlucky for me than Byron's invasion of this region, which, when I entered it, was yet untrodden, and whose chief charm consisted in the gloss and novelty of its features; but it will now be overrun with clumsy adventurers, and, when I make my appearance, instead of being a leader, as I looked to be, I must dwindle into a humble follower—a Byronian. This is disheartening, and I sometimes doubt whether I shall publish it at all; though at the same time, if I may trust my own judgment, I never wrote so well before."

Things went from bad to worse. On August 28, 1813, Byron wrote to him, "Stick to the East;—the oracle, Staël, told me it was the only poetical policy." But the letter went on to announce Byron's project of a story grafted on to the amours of a Peri and a mortal. Now, Moore had already in his long-delayed work made the daughter of a Peri the heroine of one of his tales, and spent much pains in "detailing the love adventures of her aerial parent in an episode." He wrote at once, asking only for fair warning, and Byron immediately disclaimed all commerce with Peris; but, having done so, set to work upon the *Bride of Abydos*. It is easy to judge of Moore's feelings when he read the new poem and found that Byron had again, by pure accident, anticipated his friend. One of the stories intended for insertion in *Lalla Rookh* had been carried some way, but it contained, says Moore, such singular coincidences with the *Bride*, "not only in locality and costume, but in plot and characters," that there was nothing for it but to give up.

The whole thing was pure and simple bad luck, and Byron's very sincere correspondence is mainly directed to chiding his friend for the "strange diffidence of your own powers which I cannot account for." But the blow was heavy.

There is no doubt as to Moore's priority of idea. On September 11th, 1811, we find him writing to Miss Godfrey, after the failure of his operetta, *M.P.*:

"I shall now take to my poem and do something, I hope, that will place me above the vulgar herd both of worldlings and critics; but you shall hear from me again when I get among the maids of Cashmere, the sparkling springs of Rochabad, and the fragrant banquets of the Peris." And Rogers, in the same month, refers to the projected epic: "Are you now in a pavilion on the banks of the Tigris?" But Moore, for all his apparent facility, was a slow and fastidious writer, and it seems that, even in 1813, not a great deal was accomplished.

He was, however, resolute that nothing should divert him from his task, and the proposal made by Murray through Byron, to establish him as "editor of a review like the *Edinburgh* and the *Quarterly*," was set aside; as was also the suggestion from Power for an opera, which would bring in money both from theatre and bookshops. His determination was the more remarkable, because already his account with Power was forestalled. So long as he could earn money, Moore refused persistently to be indebted to any man (except Rogers, and that only in two instances) for a loan; but with equal regularity he anticipated by long periods all his earnings from publishers. His house-moving had involved him in unlooked-for expenses, and, to meet these, he had exhausted the supply from a first success in one of the two branches of literature which he was to make peculiarly his own.

In March 1813 was published for Carpenter (through an understrapper in the Row) *Intercepted Letters; or the Twopenny Postbag*. The preface explained that the letters in question came from a bag dropped by a Twopenny Postman, which had been picked up by an agent of the Society for the Suppression of Vice, but abandoned, when it became clear that the discoveries of profligacy which it indicated lay too high up to be handled. The letters—eight in all—were attributed to correspondents whose names were transparently disguised by initials, and who for the most part belonged to the Prince Regent's circle. A supplementary group of epigrams and occasional verses, reprinted from the *Morning Chronicle*, eked out the thin volume. Thin as it was, it sold for a high price, and it sold prodigiously; a year later Moore wrote a preface for the fourteenth edition, which Carpenter now openly adopted. Moore, however, did not write in his own name. The nominal author of the preface, as of the book, was "Thomas Brown the younger." But the authorship was never for a moment in doubt, as many of the squibs reprinted had been correctly assigned on their first appearance in the *Chronicle*; and Moore showed his certitude that the disguise would be only formal by inserting, in the dedication to Woolriche, an assurance that "doggerel is not my *only* occupation." The preface to the later edition contains some biographical matter of interest. It begins by denying the rumour of collaboration or joint-authorship; and then passes to what was a virtual avowal of identity.

- 38 -

"To the charge of being an Irishman, poor Mr. Brown pleads guilty; and I believe it must also be acknowledged that he comes of a Roman Catholic family.... But from all this it does not necessarily follow that Mr. Brown is a Papist; and indeed I have the strongest reasons for suspecting that they who say so are somewhat mistaken.... All I profess to know of his orthodoxy is that he has a Protestant wife and two or three little Protestant children, and that he has been seen at church every Sunday, for a whole year together, listening to the sermons of his truly reverend and amiable friend, Dr. ——"[1]

Moore by no means conceived of tolerance only as a virtue to be practised by Protestants for the benefit of Catholics. Long before his marriage—indeed, when his Bessy was in very short frocks—he had written, as an exhortation to Protestants:—

"From the heretic girl of my soul shall I fly
To find somewhere else a more orthodox kiss?"

And later, from the Catholic side of the question, he practised his own doctrine conscientiously, when it came to falling in love, for Bessy Moore was a Protestant. In spite of the phrase "it does not necessarily follow that Mr. Brown is a Papist," there is no reason to suppose that Moore ever meditated a change of religion. Later in life, his sister Katherine did so, and he advised her to follow his example and remain quietly a Catholic. But he said openly to her, and records it in his diary: "My having married a Protestant wife gave me an opportunity of choosing a religion at least for my children, and if my marriage had no other advantage, I should think *this* quite sufficient to be grateful for."

But while in these respects he showed himself a Catholic of the least rigid order, he was, naturally, all the keener in his hostility to Protestant bigotry. And, having discarded the sonorous denunciation of Corruption and Intolerance in heavy Popian couplets, he now, as Mr. Thomas Brown the younger, attacked Addington, Eldon, Castlereagh and the rest, in a spirited light gallop of verse. The occasion of the opening epistle was afforded by a present of ponies which Lady Barbara Ashley had given to the Princess Charlotte of Wales. Lady Barbara being a Catholic, keen noses smelt Popery in the gift; and the letter attributed to "the Pr——ss Ch——e of W——s," recounts a supposed Cabinet Council, at which the crisis is discussed. A few lines may serve as an example of this clever *jeu d'esprit*.

"'If the Pr-nc-ss *will* keep them,' says Lord
C-stl-r—gh,
'To make them quite harmless, the only true way

Is (as certain Chief Justices do with their wives)
To flog them within half an inch of their lives;
If they've any bad Irish Mood lurking about,
This (he knew by experience) would soon draw it out.'
Or—if this be thought cruel—his Lordship proposes
'The new *Veto* snaffle to hind down their noses—
A pretty contrivance, made out of old chains,
Which appears to indulge, while it doubly restrains;
Which, however high-mettled, their gamesomeness checks,'
Adds his Lordship, humanely, 'or else breaks their necks!'"

The bulk of the satire was, however, social rather than political, and largely aimed at the Prince Regent—from whom Moore and all his friends were now completely estranged. In the second Letter, some capital lines describe—

"That awful hour or two
Of grave tonsorial preparation,
Which, to a fond, admiring nation,
Sends forth, announced by trump and drum,
The best-wigg'd P——e in Christendom!"

Even better work was to be found in the reprints than in the Letters. The "Anacreontic to a Plumassier" is a very delicate piece of verse, fluffy and feathery. Almost as good was the version, or perversion, of Horace II. 11, "freely translated by the Pr—ce R-g—t":—

"Brisk let us revel, while revel we may;
For the gay bloom of fifty soon passes away,
And then people get fat
And infirm and all that,
And a wig (I confess it) so clumsily sits
That it frightens the little loves out of their wits."

Taking them as a whole, it would be hard to find better examples of light-hearted satire. Moore had little of the *soeva indignatio*; his touch was on the ridiculous rather than the disgusting; and even the Prince of Wales could take fun out of the chaff directed against his fat pretensions to comeliness. Probably no one was much the worse, or the better, for Moore's satire, and it abounds so in topical allusion, of the most ephemeral kind, that to-day the interest has evaporated. But the reader can easily understand its immediate popularity, and it is distressing to think that Carpenter should have reaped the lion's share of the profit. From this onward Moore very wisely sought another publisher.

His residence at Ashbourne lasted till March 1817, and the years spent there were the most fertile of his existence. The period was terminated by a move to the neighbourhood of London to supervise the publication of *Lalla Rookh*, and virtually the whole of this poem may be said to have been composed in Mayfield Cottage. In the same period, Moore produced the sixth number of the *Irish Melodies* and the first number of his *Sacred Songs*, which rank next in importance to the *Melodies* among his poetical works. If he had never written a line after 1817, his reputation as a poet would stand no less high than it does at present.

The volume of the *Melodies* which Power issued in 1815 contains several poems which throw an interesting light on the poet's state of feeling towards politics, and especially towards his own country. One of the most successful songs in the number (as indeed it deserved to be) was the lyric in which the reproach of Catholic Ireland to the Prince who had gone back on his early protestations is put as the complaint of a forsaken woman:—

"When first I met thee, warm and young,
There shone such truth about thee,
And on thy lip such promise hung,
I did not dare to doubt thee.
I saw thee change, yet still relied,
Still clung with hope the fonder,
And thought, though false to all beside,
From me thou couldst not wander.
But go, deceiver! go,—
The heart, whose hopes could make it
Trust one so false, so low,
Deserves that thou shouldst break it."

And the closing refrain has a real energy:—

"Go—go—'tis vain to curse,
'Tis weakness to upbraid thee;
Hate cannot wish thee worse
Than guilt and shame have made thee."

Moore wrote to Power in the early part of 1815, after a visit to Chatsworth, where he had spent his days in a whirl of fine company:—

"You cannot imagine what a sensation the Prince's song created. It was in vain to guard your property; they had it sung and repeated over so often that they all took copies of it, and I dare say in the course of next week there will not be a Whig lord or lady in England who will not be in possession of it."

The other notable number is the poem to the tune Savourneen Deelish, which begins:—

"'Tis gone, and for ever, the light we saw breaking,
Like Heaven's first dawn o'er the sleep of the dead—
When Man, from the slumber of ages awaking,
Look'd upward, and bless'd the pure ray, ere it fled.
'Tis gone, and the gleams it has left of its burning
But deepen the long night of bondage and mourning,
That dark o'er the kingdoms of earth is returning,
And darkest of all, hapless Erin, o'er thee."

Moore wrote this after Napoleon had been sequestered in Elba, when the Holy Alliance were left masters of the field. He was well pleased with the verses, and his comment to Power is extremely typical of his attitude at this period:—"It is bold enough; but the strong blow I have aimed at the French in the last stanza makes up for everything." The lines referred to are these:—

"But shame on those tyrants who envied the blessing!
And shame on the light race unworthy its good,
Who, at Death's reeking altar, like furies caressing
The young hope of Freedom, baptized it in blood!"

The same desire to conciliate English public opinion is shown by another song which represents Erin as drying her tears:—

"When after whole pages of sorrow and shame
She saw History write,
With a pencil of light
That illumed the whole volume, her Wellington's name."

In one of the prefaces which Moore wrote, with ebbing faculties, for the collected edition of his works, readers will find him claiming for this lyric the spirit of prophecy, because Wellington ultimately "recommended to the throne the great measure of Catholic Emancipation." If indeed at last the Duke heeded the singer's closing injunction—

"Go, plead for the land that first cradled thy fame,"

it was with no good-will: and there is far more sincerity in Moore's note somewhere in the journals that his song had been wholly wasted on the recipient of the homage. Still, there is no good ground for bringing against the poet a reproach of time-serving. His state of mind, if one endeavours to realise it, must have been strangely complicated. In the victories of Wellington, so largely won by the bravery of Irish soldiers, he felt, no doubt, as did most Irishmen, a kind of proprietary gratification; but the dethronement of Napoleon caused him no unmixed joy. Like Byron, and many another man of that day, he had a fascinated admiration for this prodigious master of legions; and moreover, Napoleon's ruin meant the establishment of the Holy Alliance, and, as one of many corollaries, the perpetuation of helotry in Ireland. Ireland had reason to bless the movement towards liberty which came from France, and not less to execrate the excesses which strengthened the hands of liberty's opponents. There is nothing in the poem that requires defence; what requires either apology or condemnation is Moore's attempt to flavour with abuse of England's detested opponent an expression of his own convictions—involving, as they did, a condemnation of English rule.

The truth is that the business of adapting Irish nationalist sentiment to the taste of English drawing-rooms was perilous to sincerity; and, in this period of his life, Moore was steadily losing touch with Ireland. The number of the Melodies under discussion closed with the beautiful lyric in which the singer bade farewell to this way of poetry:—

"Dear Harp of my Country! farewell to thy numbers,
This sweet wreath of song is the last we shall twine."

The farewell, as it proved, was only temporary, but it indicates that Moore felt the inspiration failing him; and, as a matter of fact, the four later numbers of the Melodies are by far inferior to their predecessors. Their inferiority, however, was due to no lack of sympathy; it indicates only that the artist's instinct was right, and that Moore's thought about Ireland, in later days, took naturally other forms of expression.

But in 1815 he had been absent from his country for four long years, during which his life had been engrossed with other things; and the Catholic cause, which had always been foremost in his mind, was now losing its attraction, for two reasons, sufficiently indicated in his correspondence with Lady Donegal.

In the spring of 1815, his third child, a little girl, aged only a few months, died at Mayfield; and, in hopes to soothe the mother by change of scene, Moore decided to hasten on a long-projected visit to Ireland. Lady Donegal wrote that she heard this with regret, "for it is not a safe residence for you in any way"; and she pressed on him warnings against the "Irish democrats." Moore replied, certainly with sufficient emphasis:—

> "If there is anything in the world that I have been detesting and despising more than another for this long time past, it has been those very Dublin politicians whom you so fear I should associate with. I do not think a good cause was ever ruined by a more bigoted, brawling, and disgusting set of demagogues; and, though it be the religion of my fathers, I

must say that much of this vile, vulgar spirit is to be traced to that wretched faith, which is again polluting Europe with Jesuitism and Inquisitions, and which of all the humbugs that have stultified mankind is the most narrow-minded and mischievous; so much for the danger of my joining Messrs. O'Connel, O'Donnel, etc."

That was written in March, after the escape from Elba. A month after Waterloo, Moore put sharply enough, to the same correspondent, his detestation for the Bourbons, and his general dissent from Lady Donegal's Toryism. But, although written from Ireland, the letter expresses the sentiments rather of an English Whig than an Irish Nationalist:—

"Reprobate as I am, I am sure you will give credit to my prudence and good taste in declining the grand public dinner that was about to be given me upon my arrival in Dublin. I found there were, too many of your favourites, the Catholic orators, at the bottom of the design—that the fountain of honour was too much of a *holywater* fount for me to dabble in it with either safety or pleasure; and though I should have liked mightily the opportunity of making a treasonable speech or two after dinner, I thought the wisest thing I could do was to decline the honour. Being thus disappointed in me, they have given a grand public dinner to an eminent toll-gatherer, whose patriotic and *elegant* method of collecting the tolls entitles him, I have no doubt, to the glory of such a celebration. Alas! alas! it must be confessed that our poor country altogether is a most wretched concern; and as for the Catholics (as I have just said in a letter written within these five minutes), one would heartily wish them all in their own Purgatory, if it were not for their adversaries, whom one wishes *still further*."

Following that is a letter to Rogers, in which Moore writes of a visit to the "foggy, boggy regions of Tipperary."

"The only thing," he goes on, "I could match you[2] in, is *banditti*; and if you can imagine groups of ragged Shanavests (as they are called) going about in noonday, armed and painted over like Catabaw Indians, to murder tithe-proctors, land-valuers, etc., you have the most stimulant specimen of the sublime that Tipperary affords. The country, indeed, is in a frightful state, and rational remedies have been delayed so long that nothing but the sword will answer now."

Very similar views would have been expressed by any member of the Whig aristocracy, whose detestation of the Holy Alliance would certainly have extended itself to the Holy Water fount, and who would have shared Moore's fastidious dislike of O'Connell's method of raising party funds. It must, however, be remembered that these passages represent Moore's immature opinions; and against the description of the Shanavests as murderous savages must be set the *Memoirs of Captain Rock*, which give the natural history of agrarian crime, denouncing, not the Shanavests or Whiteboys, but the circumstances which bred such crime, as naturally and as regularly as filth breeds fever. For Moore wrote *Captain Rock* after reading Irish history and making something of an exhaustive tour through the south of Ireland, while in 1815 his sense of Irish grievances was largely theoretical. "I love Ireland," he wrote to his friend Corry, "but I hate Dublin"; and it is not very cynical to say that when he wrote this, Dublin was all he knew of Ireland. The influence of his early association with Emmet and others, renewed periodically by his visits to his home, was mainly an affair of sentiment, and spent itself during his long sojourn away from contact with Irish minds. It revived in him later, and it was nourished, by reading Irish history, into a steady conviction. But the first impulse that revived in Moore the enthusiasm for his own country was, I think, gratitude for its recognition of his services; and one may not unfairly trace something of his temporary alienation, if not from Ireland, at least from Irish Nationalists, to his feeling that his merits were not adequately valued among his own people. When he is blaspheming against the "low, illiberal, puddle-headed, and gross-hearted herd of Dublin," it is because his *Melologue* "never drew a soul to the theatres in Dublin."

In England, during these years, his reputation was at its height. Byron in 1814 dedicated *The Corsair* to "the poet of all circles and the idol of his own." Leigh Hunt the same year admitted, in his "Feast of the Poets," only four to dine with Apollo, and Moore, with Scott, Southey, Campbell, made the company. Stray pieces, such as the lines on Sheridan's death—Moore's finest piece of satire—caught like wildfire; and the *Edinburgh*, in reviewing the sixth number of *Irish Melodies*, made ample amends for its earlier onslaught. More than that, Jeffrey approached Moore, in the most honorific manner, through Rogers, to enlist him as a contributor, and a contributor Moore accordingly became.

His first article, a review of Lord Thurlow's poems, was simply a light piece of amusing criticism; but his second choice of subject astonished Jeffrey. Taking for a peg Boyd's translation of Select Passages from the patristic writings, Moore proceeded to hang upon it his views of the Fathers and their works generally. These views are perhaps a little remarkable as coming from a Catholic, and the tone of the article may be fairly inferred from a passage:—

> "At a time when the Inquisition is re-established by our 'beloved Ferdinand'; when the Pope again brandishes the keys of St. Peter with an air worthy of the successor of the Hildebrands and Perettis; when canonisation is about to be inflicted on another Louis, and little silver models of embryo princes are gravely vowed at the shrine of the Virgin;—in times like these, it is not too much to expect that such enlightened authors as St. Jerome and Tertullian may become the classics of most of the Continental Courts."

Nevertheless, even those who respect the Fathers most, will hardly deny the wit of Moore's comment: indeed, few things enable us so well to guess at the nature of his admitted brilliancy in conversation as these early articles, coming from his unjaded pen. Another quotation may be given:—

> "St. Justin, the Martyr, is usually considered as the well-spring of most of those strange errors which flowed so abundantly through the early ages of the Church, and spread around them in their course with such luxuriance of absurdity. The most amiable, and therefore the least contagious, of his heterodoxies was that which led him to patronise the souls of Socrates and other Pagans, in consideration of those glimmerings of the divine Logos which his fancy discovered through the dark night of Heathenism. The absurd part of this opinion remained, while the tolerant spirit evaporated. And while these Pagans were allowed to have known something of the Trinity, they were yet damned for not knowing more, with most unrelenting orthodoxy."

In any case, most readers will be of the same mind as Jeffrey, who wrote that he "was far from suspecting" Moore's "familiarity with these recondite subjects." But it must be remembered that Moore was always a bookish man, a poet who derived his inspiration largely from out-of-the-way literature— and this article contains references in which we see the germinal ideas of his *Loves of the Angels*. I have noted a touch of pedantry, oddly associated with exuberant youth, in his version of *Anacreon*; and something of the same combination is to be found in the *magnum opus* which, for a while at all events, set the seal upon his fame.

Nothing could more practically show Moore's position in the literary world of his day than the negotiations for the copyright of *Lalla Rookh*. In 1814 Murray offered two thousand guineas for it, but Moore's friends thought he should have more, and, going to Longman, they claimed that Mr. Moore should receive no less than the highest price ever paid for a poem. "That," said Longman, "was three thousand pounds paid for *Rokeby*." On this basis they treated, and Longman was inclined to stipulate for a preliminary perusal. Moore, however, refused, and the agreement was finally worded:—"That upon your giving into our hands a poem of the length of *Rokeby* you shall receive from us the sum of £3000." This was in December 1814. The poem was ready for publication in 1816, but that year (in the confusion after Waterloo) being very adverse to publishers, Moore generously offered the Longmans the chance to postpone or rescind their bargain; and postponed it accordingly was till May 1817.

It is worth noting that in the January of that year Moore writes to ask Power if he can "muster me up a few pounds (five or six), as I am almost without a shilling." A heavy blow had also fallen upon him, as the retrenchments then proceeding had occasioned John Moore's removal from the barrack-mastership in Dublin, with a consequent reduction of his income from £350 to £200. But the publication of *Lalla Rookh* set all right for the moment. A thousand pounds was drawn to discharge all Moore's liabilities; the other two thousand was to remain in the publishers' hands, and they undertook to pay Moore's father a hundred pounds a year as interest on it. Moore himself and his family moved up to a new house at Hornsey in Middlesex, much more expensive than his Derbyshire cottage; and here for two months he was busy with the proofs, and naturally anxious. By May 30th he was clear of all scruples as to the publisher's pockets, and with justice. A quarter of a century later Longman still looked on *Lalla Rookh* as "the cream of the copyrights."

One may take this moment for the height of Moore's prosperity. His success was emphasised by many flattering offers, one of which was to conduct a paper for the Opposition—a suggestion which Moore set aside, partly on the ground that he had lost his taste for living in London. In the middle of the first flourish of eulogy, Rogers, to whom *Lalla* had been dedicated, and who in June was housing Bessy and her young ones, carried off the poet for a trip to Paris. Moore wrote in raptures with the French capital; but that was the end of his good time.

Bad news recalled him: Barbara, the eldest little girl, was dangerously ill from the effects of a fall, and a month after his return she died. The loss fell heaviest on the mother, and it is noticeable that Moore was then the one to assume control. This seems natural enough, when one remembers that his wife was only three and twenty; but in later days, the relation was very different. The family moved for a while to Lady Donegal's house, 56 Davies Street, Berkeley Square, and thence Moore made an excursion to look for a new home. A great Whig peer, the Marquis of Lansdowne, had suggested that the poet's residence should be fixed near Bowood and its library; and three houses were offered for his inspection. Only one proved to be at all within the reach of his means, a little thatched cottage with a pretty garden. Bessy went down a week later, escorted by Power, to look at it, and returned delighted—very probably with its cheapness, for it was offered to them furnished at £40 a year. Under these rather sad circumstances, Moore and his wife moved into their definitive home. On November 19th, 1817, Moore wrote to Power from "Sloperton, Devizes," to say that they were in possession, and that he himself was just sallying out for his walk in the garden, with his head full of words for the Melodies.

It was always his habit to compose out of doors, and pilgrims to Sloperton are still shown a little gravelled path round the garden, which keeps the name of Poet's Walk. Such pilgrims can easily enough imagine the house as Moore first knew it. The thatched roof has been replaced by slates, probably when the addition was built on for Moore's accommodation. This addition consisted of two rooms, a good-sized sitting-room with windows opening on to the green lawn and garden, and over it a bedroom to match—the room in which Moore died, and which, according to tradition, his ghost still inhabits. This addition has an ordinary sloping roof, joined on to the original front, which consists of three gables. All about are great elms and chestnut trees, and the whole countryside is rich in the beauty that Moore delighted in—"sunniness and leanness," to quote his own happy phrase. The quiet little country town of Devizes is three miles off to the north, and in that direction Bromham, the hamlet which gives its name to the parish, nestles among trees across a small valley. A roughly paved lane, deep sunk between profuse hedges, leads from Sloperton to the lovely fifteenth-century church in whose grave-yard Moore lies with his wife and children, among generations of squires and yokels of a race not his own.

From this valley the ground rises gently, and the road from Devizes to Chippenham has to crest a hill or swelling ridge. Astride of the ridge is Lord Lansdowne's demesne, and from Moore's house to the nearest entry to the park, the distance must be something over a mile. Thence it is another mile's walking through glades and lawns to the great house—"dear Bowood," as Miss Edgeworth called it, famous in those days for its hospitality to men and women of letters. Altogether the neighbourhood was as pleasant as could be found, but at first Bessy Moore was uncomfortable in it. She wanted "some near and plain neighbours to make intimacy with and enjoy a little tea-drinking now and then." The Lansdownes had every wish to be kind, but they and their friends belonged to a set of which Moore had for years been a privileged member, and if Bessy entered it, she found herself, as Moore said, "a perfect stranger in the midst of people who are all intimate." She consoled herself however with works of charity, visiting the poor about her, and helping them with her clever fingers. In the meantime Moore was busy with another collection of light verse—*The Fudge Family in Paris*, for which his visit to Paris with Rogers had given the suggestion; and a seventh edition of *Lalla Rookh* was printing within less than a year after publication. Thus all omens seemed hopeful, when suddenly a bolt from the blue came down.

Moore's deputy in Bermuda had proved thoroughly untrustworthy, repeated letters having elicited no accounts from him for the last year of the war. It appeared now that he had embezzled the proceeds of a ship and cargo— representing a sum of £6000, which had been deposited with him, pending an appeal to the Court at home. Moore was fully liable, and his only hope lay in the conscience of a certain merchant, uncle of the defaulter, who had recommended his nephew to Moore, and might therefore feel bound in honour to make good the defalcation. Moore bore himself, however, cheerfully enough, though anticipating sequestration in a debtor's prison. The advice of business men in London reassured him somewhat, and the *Fudges* came out at the right moment with great éclat, bringing in £350 to the author within the first fortnight. Consolation of another kind was administered, when, in May of the same year (1818), the poet ran over to Dublin, and for a fortnight lived in a bustle of acclamation. A great public dinner was organised in his honour, and when he appeared in the theatre, he was called repeatedly during the performance to make his bow from the front of the box. All this, he said, "was scarcely more delightful to me on my own account than as a proof of the strong spirit of nationality of my countrymen."

Another great exultation helped to dispel the gloom of his Bermuda prospects, for in October Bessy became at last the mother of a son. Little comfort as this child proved to be in the long run, he was for years the apple of Moore's eye. The god-parents were, as usual, a strange and interesting assortment—Miss Godfrey, the shrewd and tried friend of so many years, Lord Lansdowne, and old Dr. Parr, the famous Grecian. This last was a recent acquaintance, sprung out of the work on which, during the year, Moore had been engaged—a new literary departure marking the incipient change in him from poet to man of letters.

His lines on the death of Sheridan showed plainly the hold which the one brilliant Irishman had on the other's imagination, and Murray suggested in 1817 that Moore should be Sheridan's biographer. By August 1818, Moore was at work, visiting Sheridan's sister, Mrs. Le Fanu, in Bath; and at her house he first met Dr. Parr, who warmed to the scholar in Moore. They talked together of Erasmus, the Wolfian theory of Homer, and such like things; hobnobbing generously the while.

Material in plenty for the Memoir was forthcoming, from a diversity of sources, but difficulties arose as to the share in the prospective profits claimed by the Sheridan family, and Moore occupied himself with other researches: reading *Boxiana*, visiting Jackson the pugilist, and studying other repositories of "flash" dialect, in order to fit himself for the task of writing his new squib *Tom Crib's Memorial to Congress*, in which a professional boxer, Crib, was the spokesman. It appeared in the spring of 1819; the seventh number of *Irish Melodies* had been issued in the preceding year, so that it will appear that Moore's industry was constant. Work on the *Sheridan* continued briskly, as we find by entries in his diary, it having been settled that Murray was to be the publisher and to pay 1000 guineas for the book. In the meantime Moore was turning over subjects for another poetical *opus magnum*, and something in his omnivorous reading suggested a story drawn from ancient Egypt—a first hint of the material which he ultimately wrought into his prose romance, *The Epicurean*.

In the summer he made his usual visit to town, and Bessy with the children went off by boat to Edinburgh to visit her mother and sisters. The Dyke family appear to have dropped pretty completely out of Moore's existence, but occasional references show that they continued to keep in touch at least with Bessy, and to receive small sums. Moore's cause was now at last up for hearing, and his sanguine nature had led him to hope for a dismissal of it: but on July 10th the blow fell. He learnt that in two months an attachment would be put in force against his person, and therefore there was nothing left for it but to decide on a place of retreat. The Liberties of Holyrood were suggested, and Moore had all but decided on going there, when Lord John Russell— most unfortunately, as he came to think—urged the alternative of a visit to the Continent in his company, with a view to final settlement in Paris. The Longmans backed the suggestion by saying that a few poetical epistles from places of note would pay all expenses; and accordingly in the beginning of September 1819, Moore set off for Dover in Lord John's coach.

This break-up of so pleasant a home was distressing, and friends were eager to prevent the necessity. Promptest of them was Jeffrey, who, immediately the report of the calamity came, made excuse for writing a letter on business of the *Edinburgh*, and then went on:

> "I cannot from my heart resist adding another word. I have heard of your misfortunes and of the noble way you bear them. Is it very impertinent to say that I have £500 entirely at four service, which you may repay when you please; and as much more, which I can advance upon any reasonable security of repayment in seven years?
>
> "Perhaps it is very unpardonable in me to say this; but upon my honour, I would not *make* you the offer, if I did not feel that I would *accept* it without scruple from you."

Nothing could be more honourable to both men than such an offer, and Moore long afterwards referred to it in his Memoir with deep feeling. It was only one of a shoal of similar tributes. Leigh Hunt, then editor of the *Examiner*, wrote to Perry of the *Chronicle* to urge the opening of a public subscription. Rogers pressed £500 of his own on Moore, as a beginning towards some such fund: Lord Lansdowne offered security for the whole; Lord John Russell proposed to set aside all future profits from his *Life of Lord Russell*, just published, and forwarded inquiries from his brother Lord Tavistock as to whether anything was doing to save Moore from imprisonment. "I am very poor," Lord Tavistock wrote, "but I have always had such a strong admiration for Moore's independence of mind that I would willingly sacrifice something to be of use to him." Moore recorded all this with legitimate pride, in his diary, but continued steadfast in his determination to rely on no one but his publishers; and the Longmans expressed the fullest readiness to advance in the way of business any reasonable sum, to which he might, by compromise, reduce the claims on him.

Nothing could more strongly indicate the general respect in which Moore was held than this practical testimony. It is necessary to emphasise that Moore impressed those in contact with him by no quality so much as by his high-mindedness. Old Dr. Parr expressed the feeling of many, when he left by his will a ring to Thomas Moore, "who stands high in my estimation for original genius, for his exquisite sensibility, for his independent spirit and incorruptible integrity." Men who saw how Moore lived felt no doubt the greatness of the temptations to which he was exposed. Private liberality was pressed upon him repeatedly; and if his pride revolted from that, he had more than a common chance of public rewards. Those anxious to serve the poet were by no means only of one political colour; no man had more aptitude to conciliate, or stronger motives for doing so. Early in his married life, at a time when his professed patron, Lord Moira, took office under a government opposed to the Catholic cause, which he, like Moore, had always supported, the poet might easily have waived something of his scruples; and Miss Godfrey insisted upon the reasons for his doing so, in language which would probably have been endorsed by most of his Whig friends.

> "As to your political opinions, it was very fine to indulge in them and act up to them while there was a distant perspective in so doing of fame or emolument, and at the same time a feeling that the triumph of such opinions, and the success of the party you belonged to, might be conducive to the prosperity of your country. But now, when those opinions have less and less influence, and that party less and less consideration—when your family is increasing

and your wants, of course, increasing with it—don't you think prudence should have its turn? Would not your love for your wife and anxiety for the welfare of your children reconcile you to some little sacrifice of political opinions?"

The same line of argument was used to Moore at many junctures in his life and he always had the same answer. "More mean things," he told Rogers, "have been done in this world under the shelter of wife and children than under any pretext that worldly-mindedness can resort to."

The fact that the argument was so often used indicates that he lived always in the range of temptation; and many would blame him because he never had the inclination to sever himself from the connections which made it almost impossible for him to live frugally. Yet, apart from the argument that he helped the popularity of his music by singing his songs as no one else could sing them, it is clear that for much of his work—for all the satirical side of it—close touch with society was essential. Hardly less essential was it for the work of which his *Sheridan* was only the first instalment—his contribution to the literature of memoirs. On the other hand, it is clear that as the satirist, the observer, the historian, and the politician strengthened in him, they crowded out the poet. Life near Bowood meant life in contact with the leading politicians and thinkers of the day: Sloperton was very different from the seclusion of Mayfield. The question naturally arises, whether Moore, by encouraging his interest in contemporary events, and, generally speaking, in the prose side of life, stifled a higher gift, or whether he simply obeyed a sound and healthy impulse. The answer cannot be given without some detailed consideration of the work by which he took rank in his own generation—his equivalent for Scott's lays and Byron's romances.

Like them, Moore relied upon the charm of an exciting narrative, laid in unfamiliar scenes, and furnished with highly-coloured descriptive passages. But, whereas Scott wrote of the Border where he had been bred, and Byron of the East where he had travelled in days when the traveller was obliged to become a real part of every scene in which he moved, Moore laid his stories in a country known to him only through books, and he derived them from a literature remote and alien from all European sympathies. The natural consequence is that, whereas Scott's and Byron's descriptions savour of actual experience, Moore's reek of the lamp; and, with astonishing lack of judgment, he spoilt whatever illusion might exist, by the constant interposition of footnotes to explain the fragments of Eastern custom, tradition, or natural history, which he had laboriously wrought in. Nothing could more strongly stamp the artificial character of the whole. The truth, which Moore unhappily did not realise, is that poetry should be made, not out of things new but of things old; out of the familiar, not the unfamiliar. His research for novelty of subject was fatal to him; the attractions which he sought to give his work are those which poetry in the true sense must dispense with. Scott handled material wrought over a hundred times in Border ballads. Byron indeed made poetry from the novel, the strange, the obviously picturesque. But what keeps Byron's poetry alive is the element of personal emotion which Byron contributed to the subject. In so far as anything survives of *Lalla Rookh*, the same is true of Moore.

The introductory pages prefixed to *Lalla Rookh* in the 1841 edition of Moore's poems bear out this view. Moore relates his difficulties—his many attempts, begun and thrown aside. In one of these rejected stories, and only one, he writes, "had I yet ventured to involve that most homefelt of all my inspirations which has lent to the story of 'The Fire Worshippers' its main attraction and interest"—that half-veiled reference to Irish history and Irish aspirations, of which mention has already been made. Moore shrewdly observes that the absence of this sort of feeling in the other preliminary sketches—

> "was the reason doubtless, though hardly known at the time to myself, that, finding my subjects so slow in touching my sympathies, I began to despair of their ever touching the hearts of others.... But at last—fortunately, as it proved— the thought occurred to me of founding a story on the fierce struggle so long maintained between the Ghebers, or ancient Fire Worshippers of Persia, and their haughty Moslem masters. From that moment a new and deep interest in my whole task took possession of me. The cause of tolerance was again my inspiring theme; and the spirit that had spoken in the melodies of Ireland soon found itself at home in the East."

It found itself about as much at home, I should say, as is the ordinary European in oriental costume at a masked ball. To wear Eastern clothes like an Eastern is possible, for one who has assimilated the Eastern way of life; otherwise, incongruities reveal themselves with every gesture. Byron, happier than Moore in his choice, wrote of an East that touches the West, of the clash between Frank and Moslem.

Worse still, Moore was an amatory poet, he had made successes by writing about love; and accordingly, he determined to rely in his poems—as Scott, wiser than he, had not done—on the love interest. He misunderstood his own temperament. Love poetry of the serious order demands passion, and Moore is the poet of dalliance, not of passion. The passion—if it can be called a passion—of pity, the passion of political enthusiasm, he had; but the violence of exclusive desire, whether lasting or temporary, which Byron so often rendered, was a chord outside of Moore's range.

The poets of Moore's own day, who knew and liked Moore, never cared for *Lalla*; and Leigh Hunt, an excellent critic, spoke the truth about it. Condemning the poem gently as "too florid in its general style," though allowing to it exquisite passages, he goes on:—

> "You are so truly, by birth, a poetical animal, out of the pale of book-associations and a free inhabitant of the most Elysian parts of nature, that the more you resolved to speak and to feel out of the sincerity of your own impulses, without thinking it necessary to search for ideas, the more to your advantage I am persuaded it would be. You are a born poet and have only to claim your inheritance—not to be heaping up a multitude of anxious proofs which, though mistaken by some for ostentation, are in reality evidences of a diffidence of pretension which you ought not to feel."

No man could give better advice. Moore had written narrative poetry, one may safely say, because the fashion of the day was for narrative. He had caught at Rogers's suggestion of poetry on an Eastern theme, which was to give him a new field. As he worked on, he felt his theme alien, and tried to make himself at home in it by taking into the subject what really belonged to another atmosphere; and further, he decided that "he must try to make up for his deficiencies in *dash* and vigour by versatility and polish." Not in this way is poetry written; the poet who tries to accommodate himself to the taste of the public is destroying his art.

Moore had earned his fame by writings, amatory, political, and satirical, which it came natural to him to produce, because he was "a poetical animal"; *Lalla Rookh* was, in great measure, work done against the grain, and relying for its success on the secondary qualities of elaborate finish, profusion of ornament, and variety of interest. These qualities, however, were present in no common degree, and the poem's success is not to be wondered at. The dose of novelty in style was just sufficient to attract, without offending by its revolt against "the Popish sing-song." It was indeed so perfectly in the fashion of its time, as to be inevitably demoded after a lapse of years. The florid loops and curves of the Regency period in decorative art have their equivalent in Moore's profuse and lengthily elaborated metaphors. Certain features of the work must be unreservedly condemned. The prose narrative in which the four poems are set is deplorable—sprightly beyond endurance; and in the *Veiled Prophet* Moore tears one passion after another to tatters in bursts of sheer rhetoric. Yet even here good lines are plenty, though they are all in metaphors, or some other excrescence; for instance—

"Hundreds of banners to the sunbeam spread
Waved, like the wings of the white birds that fan
The flying throne of star-taught Soliman."

In *Paradise and the Peri* we have a production more within the poet's range. A prettier example of an *Arabian Nights Tale*, done into springing, easy verse, it would be difficult to find. The idea, neat and graceful, could have been treated within the compass of a song, which should tell how the exiled Peri was promised admittance if she brought "the gift that is most dear to Heaven"; how she tried first the patriot hero's life-blood—(shed in vain); then the last sigh of the maiden who chose to share the death of her true love; and, last of all, how she won home with the tear of repentance from a Byronic sinner. All through the poem there is the suggestion of singing, and, as Scott said, "Moore beats us all at a song."

From "The Fire Worshippers" I have quoted already the best passages, those which express most fully the germinal idea. One may add an energetic denunciation, which had its full application, for instance, to Leonard McNally, Emmet's advocate, who defended most of the Irish political prisoners during a long period of time, and regularly sold the secrets of his defence to the Government.

"Oh, for a tongue to curse the slave,
Whose treason, like a deadly blight,
Comes o'er the councils of the brave,
And blasts them in their hour of might!
May life's unblessed cup for him
Be drugg'd with treacheries to the brim,—
With hopes, that but allure to fly,
With joys, that vanish while he sips,
Like Dead-Sea fruits, that tempt the eye,
But turn to ashes on the lips!
His country's curse, his children's shame,
Outcast of virtue, peace, and fame,
May he, at last, with lips of flame,
On the parch'd desert thirsting die,—
While lakes, that shone in mockery nigh,
Are fading off, untouch'd, untasted,
Like the once glorious hopes he blasted!
And, when from earth his spirit flies,
Just Prophet, let the damn'd-one dwell
Full in the sight of Paradise,
Beholding heaven, and feeling hell!"

Last of all, and most lavishly decorated, is the story of the Feast of Roses at Cashmere. The opening passage is a good example of Moore's high-wrought effort after Eastern local colour:—

"Who has not heard of the Vale of Cashmere,
With its roses the brightest that earth ever gave,
Its temples, and grottos, and fountains as clear
As the love-lighted eyes that hang over their wave?

"Oh I to see it at sunset,—when warm o'er the Lake
Its splendour at parting a summer eve throws,
Like a bride, full of blushes, when ling'ring to take
A last look of her mirror at night ere she goes!—
When the shrines through the foliage are gleaming half-shown,
And each hallows the hour by some rites of its own.
Here the music of prayer from a minaret swells,
Here the Magian his urn full of perfume is swinging,
And here, at the altar, a zone of sweet bells
Round the waist of some fair Indian dancer is ringing.
Or to see it by moonlight,—when mellowly shines
The light o'er its palaces, gardens, and shrines;
When the waterfalls gleam like a quick fall of stars,
And the nightingale's hymn from the Isle of Chenars
Is broken by laughs and light echoes of feet
From the cool, shining walks where the young people meet.—
Or at morn, when the magic of daylight awakes
A new wonder each minute, as slowly it breaks,
Hills, cupolas, fountains, call'd forth every one
Out of darkness, as they were just horn of the sun,
When the Spirit of Fragrance is up with the day,
From his harem of night-flowers stealing away;
And the wind, full of wantonness, wooes like a lover
The young aspen-trees till they tremble all over.
When the East is as warm as the light of first hopes,
And Day, with his banner of radiance unfurl'd,
Shines in through the mountainous portal that opes,
Sublime, from that Valley of bliss to the world!"

But one finds a more real example of Moore's poetry in this quatrain:—

"There's a beauty, for ever unchangingly bright,
Like the long, sunny lapse of a summer day's light,
Shining on, shining on, by no shadow made tender,
Till Love falls asleep in its sameness of splendour."

If one compares passages like these with, for instance, Cowper's anapaests, even in so beautiful a poem as "The poplars are felled, farewell to the shade," it will be seen that Moore helped on the extraordinary advance in poetical technique which marks the years from 1795 to the rise of Tennyson. Moore's sense of style is always faulty—witness the very next couplet:—

"This was not the beauty—*oh, nothing like this!*
That to young Nourmahal gave such magic of bliss."

But he had a fine ear for metre, and in this poem he displayed all his resources, changing the rhythm half-a-dozen times, with interpolating bursts of song.

When, in addition, we remember that the most indolent reader could never for an instant mistake his meaning—that the volume of thought was always light as compared with the faculty of expression—that every harshness was carefully smoothed away, and condensation always sacrificed to limpidity— it is not hard to understand the poem's popularity. Yet, when all has been said, the last word is that *Lalla Rookh* is a work of very secondary merit, and retains its place in literature mainly as an example of an extinct taste. Twenty years after it was written, Moore knew this, and told Longman that, "in a race to future times (if any thing of mine could pretend to such a run), those little ponies, the *Melodies*, will beat the mare *Lalla* hollow." And indeed, if it were not for the *Melodies*, nobody would now give an eye to their stable companion.

[1] Parkinson.

[2] Alluding to Rogers's poem "Italy."

CHAPTER IV
PERIOD OF RESIDENCE ABROAD

Moore's residence on the Continent lasted three and a half years, and it formed an interlude in his life, interrupting what was otherwise a very continuous texture. The period was one of relative idleness, yet by no means of rest; and although whatever he produced during it was in verse, its close found the transition accomplished, from poet to man of letters.

The interlude opened with a real holiday, which was in truth amply deserved. After a fortnight's stay in Paris, spent in seeing theatres, sights, and a deal of company, Lord John Russell and his travelling companion posted off through France to Geneva; explored the associations of Ferney under the guidance of Dumont, the translator of Bentham, and sometime tutor to Lord Lansdowne; and then set out for the Alps. The passage over the Simplon, and the sight of the Jungfrau with the sunset-flush on its snows, so wrought upon Moore's emotions that he shed tears. At Milan the travellers parted company, Lord John proceeding to Genoa, while Moore's destinations were Venice and Rome. Travelling alone, in the "crazy little calèche" which he had been advised to buy, was no joy, and he gladly reached La Mira, Byron's country house, two hours' drive from Padua. The friends met for the first time after a separation of five years, and Moore's note of the occurrence is curiously lacking in warmth. The Byron whom he had known and liked so well was a different person from the Byron of Italy. Much had happened in the interval, and with a great deal of Byron's later, and maturer, work, Moore was very imperfectly in sympathy. Nor did the Countess Guiccioli much impress him. Byron, who had put his Venetian palace at Moore's disposal, commended him to his friend Scott, who showed the traveller round the place. A day or two later Byron came to Venice, and there was much intimate talk between the two men. On the 11th of October, Moore paid a farewell visit to La Mira and the Countess; and before the poets parted, a notable thing happened. Lord Byron handed to Moore the Memoirs of himself, of which Moore had heard for the first time a few days earlier.

From Padua to Ferrara and so to Florence we trace in the Diary rather a homesick gentleman, who begins to affect the virtuoso a little, and at the time to collect notes for an epistle on the cant of connoisseurs. In Florence he found some acquaintances, and they were in shoals before him at Rome, where he arrived in the end of October. During the three weeks of his stay here, Chantrey the sculptor and Jackson the painter—to the latter of whom Moore at this time sat—were his principal associates, and he left Rome in their company. His impressions of Italy savour a little too much of second-hand ideas to be of interest. Moore had, evidently enough, no education in art and yet was so susceptible to surrounding influences that his talk was all of pictures, statuary, buildings and so forth. His judgments on the music which he heard are in strong contrast, brief and confident—the utterance of a genuine taste. But the friendship formed with Chantrey seems to have been sympathetic and lasting, based on a common interest in human character.

On December 11th Moore arrived in Paris, and 'went as soon as I could with a beating heart to enquire for letters from home.' There were none of recent date, for the beloved Tom was ill, and Bessy would not write till the crisis was over; moreover, the Longmans wrote that nothing had as yet been settled in the Bermuda business, so that a return to England was impossible. "This is a sad disappointment," Moore writes,—"my dear cottage and my books. I must, however, lose no time in determining upon bringing Bessy and her little ones over; and wherever they are, will be home, and a happy one, to me."

Meanwhile, he took "an entresol in the Rue Chantereine at 250 fr. a month," and saw a deal of society, English and French, with potentates in plenty. But it did not console him. "I have no one here that I care one pin for, and begin to feel, for the first time, like a banished man," he wrote to Rogers; and a Christmas day apart from his family only deepened his gloom. But on January 1st, 1820, Bessy and her young ones landed safely in Paris, and things began to brighten singularly. "My dear tidy girl," Moore writes, "notwithstanding her fatigue, set about settling and managing everything immediately." Chief of the things settled was a resolution not to go into society, "which was tolerably adhered to for some time";—Moore meanwhile working at his "Fudge Family in Italy," a first draft of the poetical impressions which he published ultimately as *Rhymes on the Road*. After about a month, a successful move was made to "a very pretty cottage in the Allée des Veuves," somewhere in the Champs Élysées—"as rural and secluded a workshop as I have ever had," says Moore.

Gradually, however, virtue evaporated. The poet was beset with invitations, and, moreover, he owns to a sense of depression before the task of writing, "when the attention of all the reading world is absorbed by two writers, Scott and Byron." He had also a consciousness that his poetical essays in and upon connoisseurship were not the right thing; and finally, in June, after the whole had been set up by a French printer, it was decided to suppress the publication; Sir James Mackintosh having advised the Longmans, that the incidental satire on Castlereagh and other leading members of the Government would be injurious to Moore's interest, at a time when it might be possible to induce Government to drop its share of the claims against him; and Moore himself being influenced by the wish to publish nothing new till he had something of importance to produce.

In July the kindness of friends, M. Villamil, a Spanish gentleman, and his wife, enabled the Moores to move for the summer into pleasant quarters—a little *pavillion* in the grounds of the Villamils' house near Sèvres. Here the poet, still in pursuit of an important subject, returned to an idea which first germinated in his mind after the completion of *Lalla*—the story of a Greek who goes to Egypt in search of some philosophic secret, and during a celebration of the Egyptian priestly mysteries becomes enamoured of a young girl. She proves to be a Christian, and the hero is thus introduced to the secret communion. It is of course the basis of Moore's prose romance, *The Epicurean*, but his collected works contain a considerable fragment of *Alciphron*, his first sketch of it in verse, which dates from this time. Studies for the work brought him into touch with French savants, and the more Moore read upon the subject, the less he appears to have written. But the research drew him to Paris and away from his quarters in the "pavilion"; and when, in October, the household returned to its home in the Allée des Veuves, and Moore and his wife dined at home with the little ones for the first time since the beginning of July, "Bessy said in going to bed, 'This is the first rational day we have had for a long time.'"

Lord John Russell notes penitently on this passage, that he regrets his part in persuading Moore to prefer France to Holyrood, for "his universal popularity was his chief enemy." At no time did Moore suffer so much from being lionised, for his home was in easy reach of Paris, and in Paris French and English alike pursued this celebrity. *Lalla Rookh* was then at the height of its fame; was in the East being translated into Persian, and in the West transformed into a kind of masque which a troupe of royal amateurs presented at Berlin: and Lalla's poet was naturally much courted. Further, in the close of the year, there came a missive from Byron which was a fatal encouragement to idleness and outlay. He forwarded the continuation of the Memoirs, with the suggestion that Moore should sell the reversion of the MS. The suggestion was acted on after a while, and Murray consented to advance the large sum of 2000 guineas. Meanwhile engagements accumulated, and Moore began to lose health as well as time. He went into the world more and more as a bachelor, Bessy, as always, falling into the background when expenses grew high; though, at first, in Paris he and she went about a good deal together. Nevertheless, he wrote with all sincerity on March 25th, 1821:—

> "This day ten years we were married, and though Time has made his usual changes in us both, we are still more like lovers than any married couple of the same standing I am acquainted with."

In the autumn, it was decided that Moore should come to England *sub rosa*, and try to compromise the Bermuda claims with a lump sum out of Murray's advance. He was met with dissuasion by his friendly publishers the Longmans, and it transpired finally that Lord Lansdowne had left £1000 with them to attempt a similar settlement. The kindness gratified Moore's best qualities, as well as his mild vanity, and though he declined to profit by it, he was greatly uplifted. From London he crossed to Dublin to see his parents after three years' separation—but the separation had made no breach, for Moore wrote twice every week to his mother. The visit was a short one, and he had some fears for his safety from arrest, as he had been widely recognised in Dublin. But on his return to town the publishers met him with joyful news. The chief claim had been settled for £1000, and he was free to "walk boldly out into the sunshine," and show himself up Bond Street and St. James's. Of this £1000, three hundred were extorted from Mr. Sheddon, uncle and recommender of the defaulting deputy; the rest was settled (as a compliment) out of Lord Lansdowne's money, but a draft on Murray was immediately sent him to repay the loan.

For the present, however, Moore lacked the means to move back to England, and he remained in Paris, where, in the summer of 1822, he at last settled down to a serious piece of work—his *Loves of the Angels*—"a subject," he says, "on which I long ago wrote a prose story and have ever since meditated a verse one." The work went quickly, a thousand lines were completed within two months; and in November, when the poet's friends in Paris mustered to give him a farewell dinner, allusion was made to the new poem as all but ready to appear. It was actually out before Christmas. By that time Moore was back and comfortably established at Sloperton (an intervening tenant having died seasonably), and here he found his study enlarged, his family well, and himself "most happy to be at home again." "Oh, quid solutis!"—he exclaims, recalling the lines of Horace which tell of the joy it is to shake off a load of care, and to rest after labours in a foreign land.

When the *Angels* appeared, the press was favourable, but Lady Donegal and a good many more protested vehemently against the application to profane purposes of the scriptural legend, which tells of the sons of God mating with daughters of men. Publishers are sensitive to this type of criticism, and the Longmans jumped at Moore's offer to remodel the poem, by giving it an Eastern cast, and "turning his poor Angels into Turks." Accordingly a fifth edition was produced, in which the metamorphosis was completed; but the disguise was soon abandoned, and Moore appears to have been ashamed of his concession, for in his preface to the poem in the 1841 edition, no mention is made of this recension.

The Loves of the Angels never attained to the popularity of *Lalla Rookh*, and yet it seems a much more praiseworthy composition. In the first place, Moore had chosen a subject that fell more within his range. Outside of light verse, his only themes were love and patriotism, and here we have the amatory poet indulging his genius to the full. The whole poem is about love-making—love-making *in excelsis*, and surrounded with accessories so decorative that they remove all hint of reality. One feels instinctively that the fierce accent of passion would be out of place here, and, consequently, does not censure the absence of it. His three fallen angels who meet and recall the loves for which they lost heaven, furnish three types of love-story, distinguished with all the care of a troubadour expert in *la gaye science*.

The first angel—one of a lower rank in heaven—is of look "the least celestial of the three," and, before the crisis in his story, has tasted

"That juice of earth, the bane
And blessing of man's heart and brain."

He is the one whom woman resisted—for Woman is throughout the poem all but deified; and his lady, to escape from the terrors of his love, as he comes to her after the wine-cup, steals the spell-word from him, and flies off to heaven, whither his wings can no longer follow. The second angel, a spirit of knowledge, is wooed by woman rather than her wooer, and at last is fated to destroy her with the death of Semele. Moore evidently thought that much knowledge was a dangerous thing for the sex. His ideal of womanhood is rather that depicted in the third story, of which the third angel is the subject, not the narrator. In this angel—

"That amorous spirit, bound
By beauty's spell, where'er 'twas found,"

who fell—

"From loving much,
Too easy lapse, to loving wrong,"

we may, I think, fairly trace some lineaments of Moore's conception of himself. For this seraph a gentler doom was decreed. He and his nymph are first drawn together by the snare of music, a snare even though in sacred song: for, as the poem tells—

"Love, though unto earth so prone,
Delights to take Religion's wing
When time or grief hath stained his own.
How near to Love's beguiling brink
Too oft entranced Religion lies!
While Music, Music is the link
They *both* still hold by to the skies."

The lovers meet at the altar, but they appeal to the altar to consecrate their vows. And thus the poem closes with a passage in celebration of connubial love, which, even though it perhaps seemed to Lady Donegal too bold a gloss on the text of Genesis, may very well have pleased the poet's Bessy; for we can be very certain that the poet was thinking more of Bessy than of Genesis when he wrote it. I shall quote the whole passage, which contains some lines that have hardly their equal in Moore's writings—notably the fine strain beginning, "For humble was their love,"—and, further on, the closing period which recalls, yet not by imitation, Wordsworth's scarcely more beautiful tribute to his wife:—

"Sweet was the hour, though dearly won,
And pure, as aught of earth could he,
For then first did the glorious sun
Before Religion's altar see
Two hearts in wedlock's golden tie
Self-pledged, in love to live and die.
Blest union! by that Angel wove,
And worthy from such hands to come;
Safe, sole asylum, in which Love,
When fall'n or exiled from above,
In this dark world can find a home.

"And though the spirit had transgress'd,
Had, from his station 'mong the blest
Won down by woman's smile, allow'd
Terrestrial passion to breathe o'er
The mirror of his heart, and cloud
God's image, there so bright before—
Yet never did that Power look down
On error with a brow so mild;
Never did Justice wear a frown
Through which so gently Mercy smiled.

"For humble was their love—with awe
And trembling like some treasure kept,
That was not theirs by holy law—
Whose beauty with remorse they saw,
And o'er whose preciousness they wept.
Humility, that low, sweet root,
From which all heavenly virtues shoot,
Was in the hearts of both—but most
In Nama's heart, by whom alone
Those charms, for which a heaven was lost,
Seem'd all unvalued and unknown;
And when her Seraph's eyes she caught,
And hid hers glowing on his breast,

Even bliss was humbled by the thought—
'What claim have I to be so blest?'
Still less could maid, so meek, have nursed
Desire of knowledge—that vain thirst,
With which the sex hath all been cursed,
From luckless Eve to her, who near
The Tabernacle stole to hear
The secrets of the angels: no—
To love as her own Seraph loved,
With Faith, the same through bliss and woe
Faith, that, were even its light removed,
Could, like the dial, fix'd remain,
And wait till it shone out again;—
With Patience that, though often bow'd
By the rude storm, can rise anew;
And Hope that, ev'n from Evil's cloud,
Sees sunny Good half breaking through!
This deep, relying Love, worth more
In heaven than all a Cherub's lore—
This Faith, more sure than aught beside,
Was the sole joy, ambition, pride
Of her fond heart—th' unreasoning scope
Of all its views, above, below—
So true she felt it that to *hope*,
To *trust*, is happier than to *know*.

"And thus in humbleness they trod,
Abash'd, but pure before their God;
Nor e'er did earth behold a sight
So meekly beautiful as they,
When, with the altar's holy light
Full on their brows, they knelt to pray,
Hand within hand, and side by side.
Two links of love, awhile untied
From the great chain above, but fast
Holding together to the last!
Two fallen Splendours, from that tree,
Which buds with such eternally,
Shaken to earth, yet keeping all
Their light and freshness in the fall.

"Their only punishment, (as wrong,
However sweet, must bear its brand,)

Their only doom was this—that, long
As the green earth and ocean stand,
They both shall wander here—the same,
Throughout all time, in heart and frame—
Still looking to that goal sublime,
Whose light remote, but sure, they see;
Pilgrims of Love, whose way is Time,
Whose home is in Eternity!
Subject, the while, to all the strife
True Love encounters in this life—
The wishes, hopes, he breathes in vain;
The chill, that turns his warmest sighs
To earthly vapour, ere they rise;
The doubt he feeds on, and the pain
That in his very sweetness lies:—
Still worse, th' illusions that betray
His footsteps to their shining brink;
That tempt him, on his desert way
Through the bleak world, to bend and drink,
Where nothing meets his lips, alas!—
But he again must sighing pass
On to that far-off home of peace,
In which alone his thirst will cease.

"All this they bear, but, not the less,
Have moments rich in happiness—
Blest meetings, after many a day
Of widowhood passed far away,
When the loved face again is seen
Close, close, with not a tear between—
Confidings frank, without control,
Pour'd mutually from soul to soul;
As free from any fear or doubt
As is that light from chill or stain,
The sun into the stars sheds out,
To be by them shed back again!—
That happy minglement of hearts,
Where, chang'd as chymic compounds are,
Each with its own existence parts,
To find a new one happier far!
Such are their joys—and, crowning all,
That blessed hope of the bright hour,
When, happy and no more to fall,

Their spirits shall, with freshen'd power,
Rise up rewarded for their trust
In Him, from whom all goodness springs,
And shaking off earth's soiling dust
From their emancipated wings,
Wander for ever through those skies
Of radiance, where Love never dies!"

There is nothing else in the poem at all so good as this. And even this would
gain considerably by condensation, even by simple excisions. But the writing
is consistently polished, easy, and—short of inspiration—even excellent. The
opening may be quoted for a fine example:—

"'Twas when the world was in its prime,
When the fresh stars had just begun
Their race of glory, and young Time
Told his first birthdays by the sun;
When, in the light of Nature's dawn
Rejoicing, men and angels met
On the high hill and sunny lawn,
Ere sorrow came, or Sin had drawn
'Twixt man and heav'n her curtain yet!
When earth lay nearer to the skies
Than in those days of crime and woe,
And mortals saw without surprise,
In the mid air, angelic eyes
Gazing upon this world below."

Moore had abandoned the heroic couplet, and also the anapæstic measure,
in favour of the eight-syllabled iambic, used with skilful variations of rhyme.
And it is a proof of his matured judgment, that there is none of the tendency
to melodrama which disfigures *Lalla Rookh*. He had realised that horror was
not for him to convert to beauty; he tears no passion to tatters. Indeed, in
the one instance where he plunges into a melodramatic subject, describing
the fate of Lilis shrivelled to ashes by the embrace of her lover, and her
unblest kiss, printed with "Hell's everlasting element," the vehemence is
more impressive because more restrained.

At the same time, it does not seem probable that any current of taste will
bring back either the *Loves of the Angels* or *Lalla* into popularity. Everywhere,
even in the beautiful passage on wedlock's consolations, ornament is pushed
to redundancy; there is no concentration in the style. The same looseness of
texture may be observed in Scott and Byron, but Scott and Byron have
behind their work a weight of personality which is lacking in Moore. They

are moreover closer in touch with reality than Moore, who attributes to himself in the Diary "that kind of imagination which is chilled by the real scene and can best describe what it has not seen, merely taking it from the descriptions of others." He quotes Milton and Dante as instances where this kind of imagination produces the noblest work. One can only say—and Moore would have been prompt to agree—that Thomas Moore was neither Dante nor Milton; and for poets of a lower order we want close touch with fact. Moore's gift, indeed, was not imagination. His highest talent lay, like that of Horace, in giving expression to common emotions, which belong rather to a race, or a class, than to an individual, and which are consequently very general, though not very poignant, in their appeal.

A much higher rank may be claimed for him as a writer of satiric verse than of romantic narrative. The satiric inspiration with him long outlasted the other, for the *Loves of the Angels* was virtually the last poem published under his own name.[1] But under his other incarnation, as Thomas Brown the Younger, he contributed squibs to various newspapers and issued volumes for another dozen of years. The *Odes on Cash, Catholics, and other matters*, collected in 1828, show him to advantage, and we find something of the "wonted fires" even in *The Fudges in England*, published so late as 1835, after his brain had begun to flag. But for the top of his achievement in this kind one would always turn to the volume published a few months after The *Loves of the Angels*. This was the *Fables for the Holy Alliance and Rhymes on the Road*, comprising the work which he had cast and recast so often in Paris, together with a considerable handful of occasional verses.

From this general laudation, the *Rhymes on the Road*, Moore's impressions of Switzerland and Italy, must be excepted. Nothing in them repays perusal but the "Introductory Rhymes," with their ingenious and erudite discussion of the places and methods in which poets may compose—where Moore incidentally alludes to a favourite theory and practice of his own, which he supported by the example of Milton, as well as that here cited:—

"Herodotus wrote most in bed,
And Richerand, a French physician,
Declares the clockwork of the head
Goes best in that reclined position."

There is also a good skit on the ubiquitous English tourist, which ends with the vision of

"Some Mrs. Hopkins, taking tea
And toast upon the wall of China."

But for the rest, we have serious lucubrations—a long, long way after *Childe Harold*—upon Venice, Florence, the first view of Mont Blanc, Rousseau's abode, and other such moving themes. It is a vast relief to turn to the *Fables*, of which there are eight; and if one reader thinks the first the best, with its description of all the royalties at dinner in an Ice Palace on the Neva, and the general confusion when the Ice Palace takes to melting, it is odds but the next will choose another for his favourite. Most of them have a Proem, and one may quote the Proem and part of the Fable of "The Little Grand Lama."

PROEM.

Novella, a young Bolognese,
The daughter of a learn'd Law Doctor,
Who had with all the subtleties
Of old and modern jurists stock'd her,
Was so exceeding fair, 'tis said,
And over hearts held such dominion,
That when her father, sick in bed,
Or busy, sent her, in his stead,
To lecture on the Code Justinian,
She had a curtain drawn before her,
Lest, if her eyes were seen, the students
Should let their young eyes wander o'er her,
And quite forget their jurisprudence.
Just so it is with Truth, when *seen*,
Too dazzling far,—'tis from behind
A light, thin allegoric screen,
She thus can safest teach mankind.

FABLE.

In Thibet once there reign'd, we're told,
A little Lama, one year old—
Raised to the throne, that realm to bless,
Just when his little Holiness
Had cut—as near as can be reckon'd—
Some say his *first* tooth, some his *second*.
Chronologers and Nurses vary,
Which proves historians should be wary.
We only know th' important truth,
His Majesty *had* cut a tooth.
And much his subjects were enchanted,—
As well all Lama's subjects may be,
And would have giv'n their heads, if wanted,
To make tee-totums for the baby.
Throned as he was by Right Divine—

(What Lawyers call *Jure Divino*,
Meaning a right to yours, and mine,
And everybody's goods and rhino,)
Of course, his faithful subjects' purses,
Were ready with their aids and succours;
Nothing was seen but pension'd Nurses,
And the land groan'd with bibs and tuckers.

Oh! had there been a Hume or Bennet,
Then sitting in the Thibet Senate,
Ye Gods, what room for long debates
Upon the Nursery Estimates!
What cutting down of swaddling-clothes
And pin-a-fores, in nightly battles!
What calls for papers to expose
The waste of sugar-plums and rattles!

But no—If Thibet *had* M.P.'s,
They were far better bred than these;
Nor gave the slightest opposition,
During the Monarch's whole dentition.
But short this calm:—for, just when he
Had reach'd th' alarming age of three,
When Royal natures, and, no doubt,
Those of *all* noble beasts break out—
The Lama, who till then was quiet,
Show'd symptoms of a taste for riot;
And, ripe for mischief, early, late,
Without regard for Church or State,
Made free with whosoe'er came nigh;
Tweak'd the Lord Chancellor by the nose,
Turn'd all the Judges' wigs awry,
And trod on the old Generals' toes:
Pelted the Bishops with hot buns,
Rode cockhorse on the City maces,
And shot from little devilish guns,
Hard peas into his subjects' faces.
In short, such wicked pranks he play'd,
And grew so mischievous, God bless him!
That his Chief Nurse—with ev'n the aid
Of an Archbishop—was afraid,
When in these moods, to comb or dress him.
Nay, ev'n the persons most inclined

Through thick and thin, for Kings to stickle,
Thought him (if they'd but speak their mind,
Which they did *not*) an odious pickle.

Praed himself never equalled the ease and gaiety of these admirable compositions, and their only defect as satire is that they are too gay and too good-humoured, though certainly not too respectful. Moore's shafts have no poison: there is no strength of hatred to drive home the barb. Yet the sincerity is real, and here and there the wit leaps into real poetry, as in this stanza from "The Torch of Liberty"—

"I saw th' expectant nations stand,
To catch the coming flame in turn;—
I saw, from ready hand to hand,
The clear, though struggling, glory burn."

For finish and force these productions are far ahead of the earlier verses of the *Postbag* and *Fudge Family in Paris*: they are also clear of the rhetoric which occasionally overloads the latter. But none of them quite reaches the pitch attained in the lines on the Death of Sheridan (reprinted in the 1823 volume) which were based on the report that the Prince of Wales, after repeated neglect of entreaties, sent at last a gift of £200 to the dying man, who, knowing it too late, returned the missive. A few stanzas must be cited.

"How proud they can press to the fun'ral array
Of one whom they shunn'd in his sickness and sorrow;—
How bailiffs may seize his last blanket, to-day,
Whose pall shall be held up by nobles to-morrow!

"And Thou, too, whose life, a sick epicure's dream,
Incoherent and gross, even grosser had pass'd,
Were it not for that cordial and soul-giving beam,
Which his friendship and wit o'er thy nothingness cast:—

"No, not for the wealth of the land, that supplies thee
With millions to heap upon Foppery's shrine;—
No, not for the riches of all who despise thee,
Though this would make Europe's whole opulence mine;—

"Would I suffer what—ev'n in the heart that thou hast—
All mean as it is—must have consciously burn'd,
When the pittance, which shame had wrung from thee at last,
And which found all his wants at an end, was return'd."

There is a real anger inspiring the phrase, worthy of Dryden at his best, which stigmatises the Prince's life—"a sick epicure's dream, incoherent and gross." But Moore was too easily moved by kindness, and a civil word or action from Eldon or from Canning exempted them for ever from his attacks. Except Castlereagh, in whom he saw with justice the inveterate enemy of Ireland— and that enemy a renegade from Grattan's principles—he pursued no man relentlessly, and no institution moved him to continued hatred except the Church of Ireland. "Could you not contrive," said Sydney Smith to a portrait painter at work on a head of Moore, "to throw into the features a little more hostility to the Establishment?" Enough hostility certainly was thrown into the verses which he continued for years to contribute to the papers; and he pleased himself vastly with one address to a shovel hat:—

"Gods! when I gaze upon that brim,
So redolent of Church all over,
What swarms of Tithes, in vision dim,—
Some pig-tail'd, some like cherubim,
With ducklings' wings—around it hover!
Tenths of all dead and living things,
That Nature into being brings,
From calves and corn to chitterlings."

It is not a long way from verse of this kind on this subject to the prose of "Captain Rock." The distance, no doubt, covers a descent. But it may fairly be urged that if Moore after the year 1823 was only in a secondary sense a writer of verse, and primarily occupied with prose, the reason is, not that prose was easier or paid better, but because he was increasingly preoccupied with matter which he could not handle except in prose—matter of serious controversial argument—and matter which he was impelled to handle by a growing desire to serve his own country.

[1] *Alciphron*, issued in 1839, was, as has been said, a rehandling of a fragment composed during his residence in Paris, and has in any case no importance.

CHAPTER V
WORK AS BIOGRAPHER AND
CONTROVERSIALIST

After his return from Paris to England, once the task was accomplished of seeing his two books of verse, serious and comic, through the press, Moore turned naturally to resume the *Life of Sheridan* which he had been obliged to drop during his stay on the Continent, remote from all the living sources of information. But the business of collecting material was a long one; the claims of the Sheridan family for a share in profits were not yet settled; and in the summer of 1823 Moore accepted an invitation which led to a new literary undertaking, carried through before the *Sheridan*. This was a proposal from the Lansdownes that he should accompany them on a tour through Ireland.

The party met in Dublin, and a characteristic little episode is recorded in the Diary. Moore's mother wanted to see her son's distinguished friend, but was shy of a visit from him; so it was arranged that Lord Lansdowne should be walked past the windows where the old couple sat at watch, while he and the poet waved their salutations.

On the way south Moore revived memories of his courtship by a visit to Kilkenny. "Happy times!" he notes, "but not more happy than those which I owe to the same dear girl still." Further south, alarming rumours began to come in, telling of secret organisation among the peasantry, and of the ascendency of "Captain Rock," a mysterious individual in whose name orders and threatening letters were then issued. Killarney charmed Moore with its loveliness, but we find sympathetic observations also concerning Lord Lansdowne's trouble with his Kerry tenants, occasioned by their habits of sub-letting, rearing large families, and so forth. Altogether, the Journal is written by one who sees keenly the oppression of tithes, but on all other matters wears a landlord's spectacles; and this criticism was made sharply, and with justice, in an answer to the book which resulted from this journey.

Moore came back with his head full of material, and set to work reading for a projected narrative of his tour; but after a couple of weeks, the brilliant idea occurred to him of converting it into a *History of Captain Rock and his Ancestors*. The project expanded a good deal as he wrote, and six months' work resulted in a considerable volume, of which the first part was a review of Irish history, which showed with ingenious irony how well English policy, from the first enactments of Henry II. against Irish dress, has been adapted to perpetuate the type and breed of Captain Rock. It was the first book which Moore had written in prose, and nowhere else in his prose writings was he so lavish of wit. I may cite a couple of examples.

"My unlucky countrymen," says Captain Rock (for the Captain was the nominal author of his own Memoirs) "have always had a taste for justice—a taste as inconvenient to them, situated as they have always been, as a taste for horse-racing would be to a Venetian."

"Our Irish rulers have always proceeded in proselytism on the principle of a wedge with its wrong side foremost.... The courteous address of Launcelot to the young Jewess, 'Be of good cheer, for truly I think thou art damned,' seems to have been the model on which the Protestant Church has founded all its conciliatory advances to Catholics."

The broad facts of English misrule in Ireland were not then staled by much repetition, and Moore's statement of them was read with eagerness. In execution the book was faulty, the irony being ill sustained towards the latter part, where it touched contemporary topics. But the success was brilliant, and from Almack's to Holland House Moore heard nothing but its praises. Naturally enough, it made its way in Ireland; "the people through the country are subscribing their sixpences and shillings to buy a copy," a Dublin bookseller wrote; and the Catholics of Drogheda forwarded a formal expression of gratitude, which pleased Moore the better as he "rather feared the Catholics would not take very cordially to the work, owing to some infidelities to their religion which break out now and then in it." And, in truth, the tone is throughout that of one who rather deplores the employment of tyranny to frighten Irish Catholics out of their religion than dislikes the idea of a change of faith. Politically speaking, however, the tone of the book was firm enough. Moore, like most Irishmen, had little knowledge of Irish history, and only began to read it when he had to instruct others in its lessons. Whether because of its effect on his mind, or because *Captain Rock* gave him a reputation in Ireland, which he dearly valued, as the champion of Irish liberties, it is certain that from this time onward the direction of his mind was increasingly towards Irish subjects.

He had felt the attraction earlier. A letter to Corry, written when *Lalla Rookh* was nearly completed, says: "I have some thoughts of undertaking a very voluminous work about Ireland (if properly encouraged by *patres nostri*—the Longmans), and this will require my residence for at least two or three years in or near Dublin." Nothing came of the project, which was perhaps not strongly formed; and in any case he was drawn away from it by the enforced move to France. And although one can trace, from the publication of *Captain Rock* onward, a steady bent of purpose in him to use his pen in the service of his country, he was a second time driven out of his course by an unforeseen event. In the midst of the Captain's triumphs, while editions were rapidly succeeding each other, a great stroke of misfortune fell on Moore. Byron died; and the depositary of his Memoirs was immediately plunged into a most embarrassing situation.

The case about this famous document may be briefly stated. In October 1819, Byron handed Moore the first portion of it, as a gift which would ultimately be of value; and in 1821 he sent the remainder to his friend in Paris, making the suggestion that money might be raised on it by anticipation. This was accordingly done, and, in September 1821, Murray agreed to pay two thousand guineas, and took the manuscript into his keeping. Part of this money was applied in settlement of the Bermuda claims, and in November of that year Moore signed a deed making over the property. This deed was submitted to Byron, and Byron signed an assignment of the manuscript to Murray. Scarcely was the transaction completed, when scruples were aroused in Moore by Lord Holland's saying that he wished the money could have been got in any other way. Lord Holland's objection, as Moore states it (though expressly in his own words) was, that it seemed like depositing in cold blood a quiver of poisoned arrows for use in future warfare upon private character. Moore protested against this view of the document, and Lord Holland, who had read the manuscript, could recall nothing admitting of such a description, except a passage relating to Mme de Staël, and a charge against Sir Samuel Romilly—both of which, Moore pointed out, could be omitted or neutralised in editing for publication, as he had reserved the right to do. Nevertheless, the scruple wrought in him, and in the following April (1822) he approached Murray with a request that the deed of sale should be cancelled, and replaced by an agreement converting the transaction into a loan, with the manuscript held as security till Moore should be able to repay. An agreement on these lines was accordingly drawn up, and Moore's conscience was relieved. He expresses strongly in his Diary his feeling of satisfaction that the control of the matter was again in his own hands.

In the succeeding year he appears to have arranged that the Longmans should take over the debt (and presumably the security), advancing him the means to repay Murray; and on May 13th one of the firm mentioned that the money was ready. On the 14th it was too late; news of Byron's death reached London; and that evening Moore received a note from Douglas Kinnaird "anxiously inquiring in whose possession the Memoirs were, and saying that he was ready on the part of Lord Byron's family to advance the £2000 for the manuscript, in order to give Lady Byron and the rest of the family an opportunity of deciding whether they wished them to be published or no."

Moore soon learned that Murray, immediately on hearing the news, had gone to Wilmot Horton, offering to place the Memoirs at the disposal of the family, without recognising that Moore had any voice in the matter. Moore went to Hobhouse and explained his view of the situation, which was that nothing could be done without his consent; and he substantiated his view by recalling a clause which he had inserted in the draft-agreement. This gave him a period of three months, in case of Byron's death, in which to raise the money. The agreement had never been formally completed, and the draft could not be found. But Murray admitted in principle Moore's claim, and expressed himself ready to comply with the arrangement, provided his money were repaid in full, with interest. The manuscript could then be disposed of, as Moore suggested, by placing it in the hands of "Lord Byron's dearest friend, his sister, Augusta Leigh."

From the proposal that the work should be placed at the disposal of Lady Byron, Moore dissented altogether; it would be treachery, he said (and Hobhouse agreed), to Byron's intentions and wishes. He also strongly opposed the view, put forward by Hobhouse and Kinnaird, that Mrs. Leigh ought "to burn the manuscript altogether without any previous perusal or deliberation." This, he said, was to treat it as if it were a pest-bag, whereas, "although the second part was full of very coarse things, the first contained (with the exception of about three or four lines) nothing which on the score of decency might not be safely published."

Matters were at this point on May 15th, and on the 16th a meeting took place at Murray's between Moore, Hobhouse, and Mr. Wilmot Horton and Colonel Doyle, the last two representing Mrs. Leigh. The agreement between Moore and Murray had not yet been found, and discussion was conducted on the assumption that Moore had a controlling voice in the matter. Thus, although, as it was subsequently decided, Byron's formal sanction of the assignment of the property to Murray would have rendered the later agreement inoperative, Moore has full right to praise or blame for the consent which he gave to the step taken at this memorable meeting; when, as the world knows, after a very quarrelsome scene, the manuscript was formally destroyed by Mrs. Leigh's representatives.

It does not appear that any one of the parties concerned in the act felt in the least that they were depriving Byron of a posthumous justification of his own career. Moore, in all the references to this Memoir, treats it solely as a piece of literature, and Lord John Russell, who had read most, if not all, of the composition, simply says that it "contained little trace of Byron's genius and no interesting details of his life." Those who were eager for suppression appear to have been influenced by the desire to avoid scandal; and the notion was widespread, for Moore, after the affair, was congratulated on having "saved the country from a pollution." His most serious objection to destroying the MS. rested on the support which such an action would give to this view of what Byron had written.

But the objection was not strong enough to induce him to jeopardise his own character. Moore's hands were tied in the transaction by the fact that he stood to lose two thousand guineas if the MS. were destroyed, and would avoid this loss if his own opinion, favouring publication, were adopted. Whoever opposed publication in the discussion at Murray's, had merely to hint that Moore's advocacy was interested, and pride would at once constrain the needy poet to consent to the holocaust.

The two persons who stood to lose in the matter were Moore and Murray, and both made a creditable sacrifice. Murray resigned his chances of a considerable profit. But Moore incurred deliberately a ruinous burden of debt. Even so, his sensitive conscience was not quite clear as to the justification of his act; but Hobhouse appears to have decided him by saying that Byron had more than once expressed a regret at having put the Memoirs out of his own power, and had only been prevented from reclaiming them by his dislike to taking back a gift.

Moore's need for consulting on points of honour did not end with the burning of the MS. Byron's family were anxious to repay him the money which he had paid to Murray before the cremation; and, not unnaturally, Lord Lansdowne and other friends urged him to accept. But he refused persistently to do so, though one adviser after another forced him to postpone for a week the irrevocable step of publishing his account of the transaction in the papers. His view was, that his duty had been to surrender the trust into the hands most proper to receive it, and that he could keep at least the credit of having made a sacrifice in order to do so. With this credit he refused to part; and he notes that he had little trouble in bringing his men of business, the Longmans, to take his view of the matter, but could not so easily persuade Lord Lansdowne, with Rogers and the rest, that a poor man ought to act on the same principles as if he were rich. It should be remembered to Moore's credit that he on many occasions followed his own sense of honour when he might have pleaded the advice of most honoured and honourable persons for adopting another course.

Friends of Moore's fame will rejoice that he acted in so scrupulous a spirit, but the necessity is to be deplored. The heavy load of debt thus thrown upon him forced him into producing too much. It also made it practically inevitable that he should recoup himself for this loss by undertaking the most lucrative task that offered—namely, a biography of Byron; yet he was uncertain for a considerable time whether the thing ought to be done, and, if done, whether he was the right person to do it. Even when his mind was clear of these perplexities—which Hobhouse strengthened by dissuading him from the task—there was a long period of suspense for which Murray was answerable. During three years Moore was distracted, anxious, and uneasy, unable to settle down to any important work.

For the present, however, once the Byron business was settled, his mind and his hands were full. It had been finally settled that the Longmans, and not Murray, should be the publishers of the *Life of Sheridan*; they undertaking, not only to pay Moore a thousand guineas, but to give the Sheridan family half profits, once 2500 copies had been disposed. Moore went resolutely to work, and in October of the next year the book made its appearance, and succeeded beyond expectation. The Longmans expressed their sense of its merits by adding £300 to the stipulated thousand.

The *Life of Sheridan* did not interest contemporaries mainly as a piece of biography. Many references to traits and stories of the dramatist and statesman, which occur in the Diary, make it plain that Moore had conceived an opinion of Sheridan by no means wholly favourable, and biography of the unsparing order was not a task which he would have undertaken. His aim was to outline Sheridan's career, rather than to paint the man, and consequently the book's main value lay in the historical view which it gave of the past fifty years. On this Moore was congratulated by so good a judge as Jeffrey, and he had a right to feel that his claim was established to rank with serious political thinkers.

Yet even before this, he was by no means regarded merely as a person of quick fancy and lively talent. It was proposed that he should join Jeffrey in editing the *Edinburgh*; and, still more remarkable, in 1822 the proprietors of the *Times* invited him to replace Barnes for six months in conducting their paper. Moore refused the offer (which was made at the suggestion of Rogers), but felt highly gratified; and from his return to England he was a constant contributor to the *Times*, sending there all his satiric verses. Their popularity was so great that the proprietors authorised Barnes to pay Moore a retainer of £400 a year; and up to 1828 this source of income, with the annuity from Power, was his main revenue. It was precarious, however; for the *Times* sometimes took a tone in handling Irish topics which made it difficult for Moore to continue the connection, and in 1827 he formally closed it. It was renewed, however, after Barnes made a tour in Ireland (carrying introductions from Moore), and returned ready "to support the Irish cause with all his might."

Indeed, the best work of the three years 1825-8 is to be found in the *Odes on Cash, Corn, and Catholics*, nearly all of which were contributed to the *Times*. The first "evening" of *Evenings in Greece*, and the fifth and sixth numbers of *National Airs*, which were the work done for Power at this period, have little in them but fluent verse; and even less can be said for the work which Moore took up as a *pièce de résistance*, his discarded Egyptian story, which he now completed as a prose romance. In *The Epicurean* we have the last and by no means sprightly runnings of the vein which produced *Lalla* and the *Loves of the Angels*: an imagination feeding itself on marvels read of in books, and producing literature which appealed to curiosity more than to any other instinct. The description of the Egyptian mysteries seen by the young philosopher, who goes to the land of pyramids and catacombs in search of new truth, is frigid in the extreme; and the flashes of genuine poetry which redeem *Lalla* and *The Angels* find no place in this very bad example of deliberately poetic prose. Nevertheless its oversweetened eloquence found plenty of readers, and the book realised £700 to its author,—of which, however, £500 had already been anticipated, independently of the main debt, the two thousand guineas.

One may note here a very curious scruple of literary conscience which Moore adhered to with surprising consistency. Although heavily in debt, and forced to make every penny by sheer production, he constantly set aside a means, which for at least ten years was constantly open to him, of earning money with little labour. His reputation then stood at its highest point; he was not only high in favour with the frequenters of Holland House, but also with the whole fashionable world and its far-off imitators. A single trait—which, with his usual naïve pleasure in instances of his own popularity, he records—may illustrate the matter. At a country ball, a young lady who was fortunate enough to shake hands with the poet "wrapped the hand up in her shawl, saying no one else should touch it that night." Fame of this sort is very marketable, and to-day would bring its owner big offers from the popular magazines. Their equivalent in those days was found in the annuals of the type of the *Forget-me-not, Souvenir*, etc.; and request after request was made to Moore for his name either as editor or contributor. The Longmans proposed to undertake such a publication, and tempted him with the prospects of £500 to £1000 a year if he would edit it. He replied, not with a direct refusal, but with a letter stating his views concerning literature of this class, which not only convinced the firm that he personally would injure his reputation by accepting, but decided them to abandon the scheme. Again, about 1827, Heath the engraver offered, first £500 and subsequently £700 a year to Moore if he would edit a new album or magazine, and at the same time tried to force on him a cheque for a hundred pounds as the price of a contribution of a hundred lines. But Moore was not to be tempted. Only once in his career did he depart from what his sense of the dignity of letters demanded, and that was at a time when he had brought himself low in purse by writing books to express his convictions, and refusing commissions that would have brought in large sums. His scruple, which nowadays seems strangely demoded, is the more respectable because he never hints a word of blame for those who did not share that "horror of Albumising, Annualising, and Periodicalising which my one inglorious surrender (and for base money too) has but confirmed me in." Characteristically enough, however, he did for courtesy what he so often refused to do for profit, and waived the scruple in favour of his old and beautiful friend Lady Blessington, to whom he thus expressed himself. He sent her some verses for her *Book of Beauty*, which are among the latest and by no means the worst that he wrote.

In 1827, however, at a time when nothing was yet settled as to the *Life of Byron*, his refusal of the inducements held out by Heath and the Longmans was not his only example of constancy to a point of honour. Letters apprised him in December 1826 that his father's death could not be long deferred, and when he reached Dublin the old man was too far gone to see or recognise his son. It is characteristic of Moore that he counted this to be a great relief, "as I would not for worlds have the sweet impression he left upon my mind when I last saw him exchanged for one which would haunt me, I know, dreadfully through all the remainder of my life." This morbid shrinking from actual physical impressions of pain or horror was a marked trait of the man, and not a manly one; it was doubtless closely connected with his temperamental liability to uncontrollable bursts of emotion. Nevertheless it was a thing hardly more within his will-power than is the common tendency to turn faint at the sight of blood; and in other respects he made up for it by exhibiting a noble staunchness. The death of his father was a heavy blow, as making the first gap in a family so closely linked by affection; but a man at forty-seven must be prepared to lose his parents, and the actual trouble of so quiet a death in the fulness of age would soon have passed naturally. But John Moore's pension died with him, and his son, already sufficiently embarrassed, found his mother and sister added to his other charges. The burden could have been avoided; for Lord Wellesley, then Viceroy, at once signified a wish to continue the half-pay pension to Moore's sister, out of a fund which he, as Lord-Lieutenant, could dispose of without reference to England, where the King might reasonably be presumed unfriendly to such a favour. "All this," Moore notes, "very kind and liberal of Lord Wellesley; and God knows how useful such an aid would be to me, as God alone knows how I am to support all the burdens now heaped upon me; but *I could not* accept such a favour. It would be like that *lasso* with which they catch wild animals in South America; the noose would only be on the *tip* of the horn, it is true, but it would do."

He found himself again approved in his action by men of business (Power the publisher and various Irish friends) but censured by Lord Lansdowne. His answer was ready, however. *The Life of Sheridan*, with its outspoken strictures on certain passages in Whig policy, had not been altogether relished at Bowood, and Moore was for once not sorry, since the lack of approbation proved the independence of his attitude. And it was now easy for him to say that, since Lord Lansdowne had described his last published book as too conciliatory to the Tories, any favour coming to its author from a Tory government would certainly be construed by unfriendly judges as the price of this civility.

At last, however, the long negotiations about Byron's Life and Letters came to a conclusion. Moore, whose debt was to the Longmans, and who was moreover bound to them by gratitude for much real friendliness, inclined to write the *Life* for them, and an arrangement to that effect was made. But in February 1828, when Murray, who held the great bulk of the material, finally made up his mind to secure Moore's services, if possible, both as editor and biographer, the Longmans, with their accustomed liberality, waived their claim. It was settled that Moore should receive 4000 guineas, of which sum half was to be advanced, to pay off his debt to the Longmans. And thus, after many efforts, he got, for a time at least, level with the world.

The work once undertaken went on fast—Moore working, he writes, "as hard as it is in my nature to work at anything"—and by the end of 1829 the first of two quarto volumes was ready for publication. In his prefatory note to the second volume, which shortly followed, Moore—whom Byron called "the only modest author he had ever known"—attributed the success of the work to the interest of the subject and the materials. There is no denying that his modesty was in this case justified. The *Life of Byron* has probably been more read than any biography in the language, with the single exception of Boswell's; yet it has no claim to rank, for instance, with Lockhart's masterpiece as a literary achievement. Moore's task was simply to weave together a chain of narrative from the copious materials presented to him by the poet's journals, letters, and, not least, by his poems. His work was, however, hampered by the necessity of sparing sensibilities, and we have frequently to wish that he had been less discreet. Nevertheless, upon the whole, a very difficult undertaking was carried through with supreme tact, with well-practised dexterity, and, above all, with a most commendable absence of pretension. Beyond the skilled selection and grouping of materials, Moore's part is very considerable. It amounts to a very acute exposition of the Byron whom he had known—a man wholly unlike the popular conception of him. Naturally enough, the work has the character of a defence or justification, and as such it is loyal and sincere. Moore never goes back on his friend. But there were in that friend's character certain elements which he disliked, and in his intellect ranges which he did not fully comprehend; and we feel always that the Byron whom Moore best understands is the Byron of earlier days, the writer of vehement romance and impassioned soliloquy—a Byron who had not yet come to the full scope of his powers. This also was natural enough, for Moore's personal intercourse with Byron practically ended when Byron married.

Their friendship began, drolly enough, as has been already mentioned, out of a cartel resulting from another challenge. In 1809, Moore saw *English Bards and Scotch Reviewers*, and had no special cause to quarrel with the attack upon his own work. Little,

"The young Catullus of his day,
As sweet, but as immoral, in his lay,"

might regard the attack as verging on a tribute; and indeed Little's poems were among Byron's earliest favourites and models in verse. But Moore was choleric; he did not like to hear himself entitled the "melodious advocate of lust"; and further on he came upon a passage which touched him on a sensitive point. His abortive duel with Jeffrey furnished too obvious material for the satirist to miss—above all, when Jeffrey was the special mark—and accordingly Moore found the following reference to it:—

"Can none remember that eventful day,
That ever glorious, almost fatal fray,
When Little's leadless pistol met the eye,
And Bow Street's myrmidons stood laughing by?"

A note was appended, stating that, in the duel at Chalk Farm, "on examination, the balls of the pistols were found to have evaporated."

The satire being anonymous, Moore, though sufficiently vexed, took no steps; but when a second edition was issued with Byron's name, he wrote from Ireland to the author, saying that in the note "the lie was given" to his own public statement, published in the *Times* concerning the duel, and demanding to know whether Byron would "avow the insult."

This letter, as Moore soon learnt, had not reached its address, for Byron had gone abroad; but he was told that Hodgson had undertaken to forward it. Nothing more was heard, and Moore let things rest till a year and a half later, when Byron returned from abroad. Moore had in the meantime married, and was about to become a father; he was therefore, as he admits, inclined to be conciliatory, but none the less determined to push the matter to an explanation. Referring to the previous letter, which he assumed to have miscarried, he re-stated his grievance in writing, but then continued:—

"It is now useless to speak of the steps with which it was my intention to follow up that letter. The time which has elapsed since then, though it has done away neither the injury nor the feeling of it, has in many respects materially altered my situation; and the only object which I have now in writing to your Lordship is to preserve some consistency with that former letter, and to prove to you that the injured feeling still exists, however circumstances may compel me to be deaf to its dictates at present. When I say 'injured feeling,' let me assure your Lordship that there is not a single vindictive sentiment in my mind towards you. I mean but to express that uneasiness under (what I must consider to be) a charge of falsehood, which must haunt a man of any feeling to his grave, unless the insult be retracted or atoned for."

Byron answered stiffly enough, that he had never seen Moore's denial, and therefore had never intended "giving the lie"; but that he could neither retract nor apologise for a charge of falsehood which he never advanced. He was ready, he said, "to accept any conciliatory proposition which did not compromise his own honour"—or, failing that, to give satisfaction. Moore, in his account of the affair, admits freely that he had shown a want of tact in talking of friendly advances, while demanding an explanation; and he expresses his admiration for Byron's conduct in the difficulty. It is certain that the younger man showed more sense and less inclination to take offence, and the final proposal that a friendly meeting should be arranged was Byron's. The place fixed on was Rogers's table, and Campbell was of the company; and the dinner (though complicated by Byron's unexpected wish to dine on biscuits and soda water—neither of which was forthcoming) had the happiest results. Byron formed a lasting friendship with Rogers; but between him and Moore an intimacy of the closest kind ripened rapidly— the more so because Byron's state was then one of considerable isolation. A few months later, the blazing success of *Childe Harold* only confirmed the friendship, as it made the new poet the lion of a society where Moore's position was already firmly fixed. Jealousy was none of Moore's vices, or he had ample ground for it in that sudden leap past him, into a region of fame which, as he always knew in his heart, he could never occupy. But even a jealous nature might have been conciliated by Byron's frank enthusiasm. "I am too proud of being your friend," he wrote, "to care with whom I am linked in your estimation"; and the fragmentary "Journal" which he kept in 1813 expresses the grounds of his admiration very fully.

"Moore has a peculiarity of talent, or rather talents—poetry, music, voice—all his own; and an expression in each, which never was, nor will be, possessed by another. But he is capable of still higher flights in poetry. By the bye, what humour, what—everything, in the 'Post Bag'! There is nothing Moore may not do, if he will but seriously set about it. In society he is gentlemanly, gentle, and, altogether, more pleasing than any individual with whom I am acquainted. For his honour, principle, and independence, his conduct to...[1] speaks 'trumpet-tongued.' He has but one fault—and that one I daily regret—he is not *here*."

Byron had also, what was no impediment in such a friendship, a great admiration for his friend's work, and his letters teem with inquiries after the progress of *Lalla*. Moore's abandonment of the story which resembled too closely the *Bride of Abydos*, he thought unnecessary, and was sincerely grieved to have stood in the light. Indeed, it is sufficiently evident that Byron's feeling for Moore was a good deal warmer than Moore's for Byron; not unnaturally, considering that Moore was newly married and deep in love with his wife. Byron is always the more frequent correspondent; it is he who has to reproach the other with slackness. But, it must be insisted again, the friendship had been begun when Moore was already rich in friendships and happy in a home, while Byron was moody and lonely in a world against which he cherished grievances; and this new companionship filled a large space in his life. The sympathy between the two is easily understood, if one remembers not only that each in his way exercised an extraordinary attraction for men as well as women, but that their tastes coincided. The days when Moore knew Byron well were Byron's period of dandyism, and Moore was always something of a dandy. Both belonged to Watier's, the dandies' club *par excellence*, and, being the only persons in the set who were men of letters as well as men of fashion, they were naturally drawn together. Moore's removal from town, too, detracted in no way from their intimacy, since whenever he returned to London, he came now as a bachelor. In 1814 they were almost daily together during his stay, and the letters give us pleasant hints of their joint festivities, from fine assemblies to lobsters and brandy and water at Stevens's in Bond Street. Their friendship was so close that it permitted of Moore's advising Byron not only to marry, but to make a particular choice—and one other than that which he disastrously made. Further, when the choice had been made, it was to Moore that Byron confided first his rejoicings and afterwards something of his perplexities.

Nevertheless Byron's marriage ended their comradeship, and the friends did not meet in the months when Lady Byron's unexplained departure and obdurate silence loosed a storm of obloquy on her husband. Moore was quick in sympathy, and Byron wrote him a letter such as could only be written to a trusted intimate. And when finally his departure was fixed on, verse spoke his feelings much better than the rather pompous dedication in prose which he had prefixed to the *Corsair* in January 1814:—

"My boat is on the shore
And my bark is on the sea;
But before I go, Tom Moore,
Here's a double health to thee.

"Were't the last drop in the well
As I gasped upon the brink,
Ere my fainting spirit fell,
'Tis to thee that I would drink.

"With that water, as this wine,
The libation I would pour
Should be—peace with thine and mine
And a health to thee, Tom Moore."

Of their meeting in Italy, three years after this was written, something has been already said. To the end of the chapter Byron was the more constant correspondent of the two. There are not wanting in Moore's Diary remarks respecting Byron in which other things than liking can be perceived; sharp disapprobation (and merited) for his writing to Murray details of a Venetian intrigue which would enable the woman to be identified; and later, a distinct touch of spleen occasioned by the disparaging estimate of all recent poetry which Byron paraded in his controversy with Bowles. Yet these are only hints of a passing mood, and it is clear that Moore was always proud of the friendship; he is quick to write down Lord Clare's assurance (which is supported by a letter of Byron's own) that Clare and he were the people whom Byron cared most for. It is also most clear that Byron's death, incurred in the cause of a nation's freedom, set him on a pinnacle in Moore's estimation, and, in the eyes of that always generous critic, more than redeemed whatever was amiss in his career. The *Life* did effectively what it was meant to do: it presented a favourable view of Byron's character, all the more convincing because the means used were chiefly quotations of Byron's own words. It is a great praise in a task so difficult to say that Moore never offends us; and on many occasions his comment is not merely sane and generous, uniting the tolerance of a man of the world with the insight of a poet; it is also instinct with dignity. For an excellent example of such moments, and of Moore's prose style at its best, the conclusion of the memoir may be given:—

> "The arduous task of being the biographer of Byron is one, at least, on which I have not obtruded myself: the wish of my friend that I should undertake that office having been more than once expressed, at a time when none but boding imagination could have foreseen much chance of the sad honour devolving to me. If in some instances I have consulted rather the spirit than the exact letter of his injunctions, it was with the view solely of doing him more justice than he would have done himself; there being no hands in which his character could have been less safe than his own, nor any greater wrong offered to his memory than the substitution of what he affected to be for what he was. Of any partiality, however, beyond what our mutual friendship accounts for and justifies, I am by no means

conscious; nor would it be in the power, indeed, even of the most partial friend to allege anything more convincingly favourable of his character than is contained in the few simple facts with which I shall here conclude—that through life, with all his faults, he never lost a friend;—that those about him in his youth, whether as companions, teachers, or servants, remained attached to him to the last;—that the woman, to whom he gave the love of his maturer years, idolises his name; and that, with a single unhappy exception, scarce an instance is to be found of any one, once brought, however briefly, into relations of amity with him, that did not feel towards him a kind regard in life and retain a fondness for his memory.

"I have now done with the subject, nor shall be easily tempted into a recurrence. Any mistakes or misstatements I may be proved to have made shall be corrected;—any new facts which it is in the power of others to produce will speak for themselves. To mere opinions I am not called upon to pay attention—and still less to insinuations or mysteries. I have here told what I myself know and think concerning my friend, and now leave his character, moral as well as literary, to the judgment of the world."

No sooner was the work on Byron completed than the prospect of another, no less lucrative, offered itself. A proposal was made, with Lady Canning's approbation, that Moore should write the Life of Canning. "The importance of the period, the abundance of the materials I should have to illustrate it, and my general coincidence with the principles of Canning's latter line of politics," as well as the money, all tempted Moore greatly, but he decided against it for a characteristic reason.

"An obstacle presented itself in the person of Lord Grey, of whose conduct, during the period in question, it would be necessary to speak with such a degree of freedom as both my high opinion of him, and my gratitude to him for much kindness, would render impossible. If left to myself, I might perhaps manage to do justice to all parties without offending any; but under the dictation of Lady Canning the thing would be impracticable."

The scruple was honourable, but it illustrates the growing difficulty of Moore's position. Bound by ties of long alliance to the Whigs, he was, in reality, less and less at one with either English party; and he claimed and exercised a perfect freedom of expression in so far as principles at least were concerned. But his regard for persons constantly hampered him, and, conscious of this personal loyalty, he did not cease to consider himself as one having claims on party rewards. Lord Lansdowne came into office under the coalition in 1827, and the Whig party were fully in power from 1830 onwards; yet Moore went unrewarded, and a trace of bitterness is clearly perceptible in his tone. Were it not that from 1829 onwards the Diary has been a good deal expurgated by its editor, we should probably hear more of this note. We have no direct expression of Moore's feelings either on the Act emancipating the Catholics or on the Reform Bill. It is sufficiently evident, however, from other passages, that Moore deprecated the tumultuary agitation by which the Duke of Wellington was persuaded to reverse the traditional policy of his party; it is probable that he considered the surrender as none the Less ignominious because he rejoiced to see it made. As to Reform, we have his mind plainly enough given in several later jeremiads. "We are now hastening to the brink with a rapidity which, croaker as I have always been, I certainly did not anticipate." That is again and again the burden of his song, and again and again he deplores that concessions were made in block, and not doled out by minimum doses. As Lord John Russell neatly observes, had Reform never passed, Moore would have lived and died a staunch Reformer. But the passing of Reform showed him for what he really was—an Irish politician of Grattan's school, hostile to every kind of Radicalism, but strong in defence of two things—the principle of religious toleration and the principle of nationality.

The result of all this was to associate Moore increasingly, both as student and politician, with Irish controversy and Irish personages. He declined to write the Life of Canning because it would necessitate personal criticism on Lord Grey, and he felt no call to give utterance to this criticism. But when it came to a question of speaking or holding his peace on the subject of his own country, Moore declined to be influenced by personal considerations. Once free to choose a subject, his choice is notable. Having declined the Canning proposal, he set to work immediately on a very different theme, the *Life of Lord Edward Fitzgerald*, and worked on it with enthusiasm, although the hope of a lucrative success was in this case slight indeed. More than that, as the Whig party settled down to the task of administration, they found, as usual, trouble in Ireland; and first Lord Holland, then Lord John Russell, urged Moore to let alone the biography of an Irish rebel till such time as Ireland should be quiet. Moore answered that this would be to rival the rustic in Horace, who waited till the stream should be done flowing by; and further, that it was a question of principle with him to publish. Lord Lansdowne's considerate silence weighed more with him than these intercessions, but the book came out in July 1831, with little of the éclat to which its author was now accustomed. It is nevertheless the best of his prose writings, and conveys with great moderation the essential truths about the series of measures and events which led up to the terrible crisis of 1798. What is still better, it gives an extremely vivid impression of the young rebel chief, who had much that specially endeared him to Moore in his warm and impulsive affections and his very generous nature. There was nothing in the subject outside Moore's sympathy or comprehension, and this was scarcely true either in the case of Sheridan or of Byron.

No sooner was this work out of hand than a new one was put on the stocks, arising again directly out of Moore's tastes and pre-occupations. This was the very curious *Travels of an Irish Gentleman in search of a Religion*, which leads naturally to some discussion of Moore's own beliefs.

We have seen that he went to college as a Catholic (though not without some consideration of the other possibility), and was thus shut off from the rewards of proficiency; but also that, while in college, he abandoned the practice of confession and that his intimates were mainly Protestants. More than this, he married a Protestant, and allowed the children of the marriage to be brought up in their mother's religion, and for a considerable period attended church with his family—as is proved by various entries in the Diary down to 1824, or thirteen years after his marriage. And in 1825 there occurs this curious note. Lord Lansdowne, referring to a magazine article, in which Moore's songs were mentioned, said, "They take you for a Catholic." "I answered," Moore writes, "they had but too much right to do so."

It is evident that his Catholicism was, to say the least of it, unobtrusive in these days; and, although a note in the journals of travel mentions the effect always produced on him by the celebration of Mass, he seems rather inclined to endorse the distaste for so much gaudy ceremonial which his Bessy owned to when first he took her to a Catholic service. The most important passage, however, bearing upon his views occurs in his account of the family interview after his father's death:—

> "Our conversation naturally turned upon religion, and my sister Kate, who, the last time I saw her, was more than half inclined to declare herself a Protestant, told me she had since taken my advice, and remained quietly a Catholic.... For myself, my having married a Protestant wife gave me an opportunity of choosing a religion, at least for my children, and if my marriage had no other advantage, I should think this quite sufficient to be grateful for. We then talked of the differences between the two faiths, and they who accuse all Catholics of being intolerantly attached to their own would be either ashamed or surprised (according as they were sincere or not in the accusation), if they had

heard the sentiments expressed both by my mother and sisters on the subject."

Taking all these things into account, I think it is not unfair to put an autobiographical construction on the *Travels of an Irish Gentleman*—which, although dedicated to the People of Ireland as a "defence of their ancient national faith by their devoted servant the Editor of 'Captain Rock's Memoirs,'" is, like that earlier work, couched in a tone of irony, and opens with a "Soliloquy up Two Pair of Stairs:"—

> "It was on the evening of the 16th day of April, 1829—the very day on which the memorable news reached Dublin of the Royal Assent having been given to the Catholic Relief Bill—that, as I was sitting alone in my chambers, up two pair of stairs in Trinity College, being myself one of the everlasting 'Seven Millions' thus liberated, I started suddenly, after a few moments' reverie, from my chair, and taking a stride across the room, as if to make trial of a pair of emancipated legs, exclaimed, 'Thank God! I may now, if I like, turn Protestant.'"

It would be wrong to say that Moore, after emancipation had freed him "not only from the penalties attached to being a Catholic, but from the point of honour which had till then debarred me from being anything else," seriously contemplated a change of religion. I think, however, that on examining his consciousness, he found that up till this period he had defended his religious position to himself solely by the point of honour, and that, now the point of honour was removed, he felt it incumbent on him to be able to speak with his enemies in the gate. I believe also that the effect of his reading was to substitute for a somewhat vague Christianity a definite attachment to Catholicism. His earlier attitude of mind is well expressed by the following passage in his Diary—not the only one of its kind:—

> "I sat up to read the account of Goethe's *Dr. Faustus* in the *Edinburgh Magazine*, and before I went to bed experienced one of those bursts of devotion which perhaps are worth all the churchgoing forms in the world. Tears came fast from me as I knelt down to adore the one only God whom I acknowledge, and poured forth the aspirations of a soul deeply grateful for all His goodness."

That was written in Paris some five years before the conversation with his sister Kate. It seems to me improbable that, after the reading and writing which went to the *Travels of an Irish Gentleman*, he would have expressed himself quite in the same way as to the advantage of being able to make his children Protestants. And it is certain that in later life, though on the friendliest terms with the rector of his parish, he never attended service at the church.

The intention of the *Travels* was, however, rather to furnish a weapon than to establish faith. In a passage of the Diary (which, by the way, deprecates the complete identification of himself with his hero), he says:—

> "My views concerning the superiority of the Roman Catholic Religion over the Protestant in point of antiquity, authority, and consistency agree with those of my hero, and I was induced to put them so strongly upon record from the disgust which I feel, and have ever felt, at the arrogance with which most Protestant parsons assume to themselves and their fellows the credit of being the only true Christians, and the insolence with which weekly from their pulpits they denounce all Catholics as idolaters and anti-Christ."

In short, this book, which he speaks of in a letter to Sir William Napier, his friend and neighbour, as "purely the indulgence of a hobby," was designed rather to annoy than to persuade. It was the attempt of an Irish Catholic, who felt increasingly his right and power to speak for his nation, to retort upon uncivil opponents not merely with argument but with derision. And for this purpose no plan could have been more effectual than the one which he chose of setting his young gentleman in the first instance, after his decision to be a Protestant, to search for the one true Protestantism.

Further than this it is unnecessary to go into the consideration of a forgotten piece of polemics, which only those will read who find, like Moore himself, "no subject so piquant as theology." His attainments in this branch of learning were considerable for a layman. We have seen that in 1814 he surprised Jeffrey by his article for the *Edinburgh* on the Fathers of the Early Church; and in 1831, while the *Travels* were in preparation, Murray astounded Milman by revealing to him that Moore was the author of an article on *German Rationalism*. Moreover, these appear to have been the only two of Moore's numerous contributions to the Whig quarterly in which he took pleasure. Reviewing, in the ordinary way, he describes as "work which I detest, and in consequence always do badly." But recondite learning always had a fascination for him, and the scholar in him grew with years.

The scholarly taste for historical research was unhappy in one of its consequences. As early as 1829, the Longmans projected a group of histories of the British Isles, in which England was to be treated by Sir James Mackintosh in three volumes, while Scott and Moore sketched, in a volume apiece, the story of their respective countries. Lord John Russell observes judiciously that had Moore kept to the restriction, the result might have been an easy, agreeable, and readable work. Unluckily, however, he obeyed rather his sense of what was needed in a history of Ireland than a perception of what he himself was fit to do, and the task, undertaken with alacrity, became a burden. Instead of one volume, it dragged out to four, of which the first appeared in 1835, and the last in 1846; and the work is wholly devoid of any original merit, bald and colourless. "His time," says Lord John, "was absorbed by it, his health worn, and his faculties dragged down to a wearisome and uncongenial task."

Yet this is to blame unreasonably Moore's choice of a subject. The truth is that, when he engaged on it, his mind had lost its elasticity and freshness of invention, from a variety of circumstances which must be considered in a review of the last period of his life.

At the same time, it was an honourable end to that long literary career. The easy singer of light loves closed his ceaseless activities with a long period of drudgery, spent, says Lord John Russell, in "the critical examination of obscure authorities upon an obscure subject." But the obscure subject was the history of the singer's own country, and Moore was at least well justified in holding that urgent need existed for spreading among the English, and still more among the Irish, a knowledge of the history of Ireland.

[1] Probably Lord Moira. *See* above, p. 55.

CHAPTER VI
THE DECLINE OF LIFE

I have now sketched to its close the later period of Moore's literary career; there remains to be set out the sad list of domestic troubles under which his health and intellect finally gave way. But first, it is pleasant to dwell upon some of the brighter circumstances which made middle age for him not the least enjoyable period of a life rich in enjoyment—and above all upon the indications, which he so highly valued, of Ireland's growing enthusiasm for her own poet.

Moore liked always "digito monstrari et dicier, 'Hic est'"; and his Journal abounds with records of his ingenuous satisfaction in such tributes. Here is an agreeable passage, which brings not only the little poet, but his very adoring (and adorable) wife, before us:—

> "Oct. 15, 1829. To Bath with Bessy, to make purchases, carpets, chimney pieces, etc., etc. In the carpet shop (in Milsom St.) where I gave a cheque for the money, and my signature betrayed who I was, a strong sensation evident through the whole establishment, to Bessy's great amusement; and at last the master of the shop (a very respectable-looking old person), after gazing earnestly at me for some time, approached me and said, 'Mr. Moore, I cannot say how much I feel honoured, etc., etc.,' and then requested that I would allow him to have the satisfaction of shaking hands with one 'to whom he was indebted for such etc., etc.' When we left the shop, Bessy said, 'What a nice old man! I was very near asking him whether he would like to shake hands with the poet's *wife* too.'"

A far more conspicuous instance, however, of his "friendly fame" is afforded by the narrative of his expedition to Scotland, in the autumn of 1825, when the publication of his *Sheridan* entitled him to a holiday, and Bessy insisted that he should take one. The purpose of the journey was to visit Sir Walter Scott, whom Moore had only once met, some twenty years earlier. There was no other guest in the house at Abbotsford, and Sir Walter, as Lockhart testified afterwards, enjoyed having Moore to himself, and gave up his mornings, usually sacred to work, in honour of the occasion. The liking between the two men was immediate, but none the less profound; and on the third day, the Diary notes that Scott said, "laying his hand cordially on my breast, 'Now, my dear Moore, we are friends for life.'" Neither friend had ever power to serve the other, but there is no passage in Moore's memoirs more evidently sincere than that in which he expresses (only a few months later) his "deep and painful sympathy" in the news of Scott's financial misfortune:—"For poor devils like me (who have never known better) to fag and to be pinched for means, becomes, as it were, a second nature; but for Scott, whom I saw living in such luxurious comfort, and dispensing such cordial hospitality, to be thus suddenly reduced to the necessity of working his way, is too bad, and I grieve for him from my heart."

But in 1825 all went gaily at Abbotsford, and Scott lionised his guest with enthusiasm—Jeffrey helping. In the Law Courts at Edinburgh Moore found himself "the greatest show of the place, and followed by crowds"; but the main demonstration took place when Scott conducted his guest to the theatre, and the whole pit immediately rose at them. Moore was compelled to bow his acknowledgments for two or three minutes, and the orchestra played Irish melodies after each act; all this to the vast delight of Scott, who, just fresh from cordialities in Ireland, was glad to see his countrymen return the compliment.

But it was in Ireland itself that Moore found himself fêted and honoured with a kind of welcome such as seldom has been accorded to any man of letters. In 1830, the research for reminiscences of Lord Edward Fitzgerald gave him a reason to cross to Dublin for a long visit, and take his wife and boys to see his mother. Here, for the first and only time, Moore made a public appearance before a gathering of his countrymen assembled for a political purpose. A meeting had been called to celebrate the recent Revolution in France, and the poet was set down to second one of the resolutions. Eloquence was one of his accomplishments, and he appears to have enjoyed the excitement of feeling that "every word told on his auditory," who overwhelmed him with applause.

The meeting had special significance, as marking a definite political connection, which the character of his book on Lord Edward only emphasised when it came to be published. He had been brought into close touch with the leading Repealers, and expressed a general approbation of their objects—though he thought O'Connell's agitation for Repeal both premature and ill-judged. He was, in truth, hardly more in complete sympathy with the Irish leader than with his Whig friends, who seemed to display in office (which they now held) all the qualities which he had disliked in their predecessors. In Ireland, however, there was every disposition to minimise differences of opinion, and the public enthusiasm for his character and achievements expressed itself, in 1832, by an effort to induce him to enter Parliament.

Moore replied with a refusal, on the ground that his means were narrow and precarious, and that he could not spare the time; as indeed he might well say, for in this year he had been forced, not only to accept Marryat's offer of £500 for contributions to a magazine, but even to borrow (for the second time in his life) from a friend, Rogers.

Curiously enough, a second proposal of the same kind came to him from a very different quarter. Lord Anglesey, then Viceroy, conveyed through a third person his wish that Moore should stand for Dublin University, and promised him all the Government support. In declining this offer on the same grounds as he had alleged to the Limerick electors, Moore added a very plain statement that, with the views he entertained, he could not enter parliament under the sanction of that Government. The Whigs had resorted to coercion, and "As long," he wrote, "as the principle on which Ireland is at present governed shall continue to be acted on, I can never consent to couple my name, humble as it is, with theirs."

The matter dropped then, so far as Government was concerned. But the Limerick constituency was not so easily put off, although Moore had explained to O'Connell—who was anxious to have the poet's support—that he should never think of entering parliament except as a purely unfettered representative. Such was the eagerness, that a scheme was formed of purchasing an estate worth £300 a year in the county, and presenting it to the poet; and after this proposal had been communicated by letter, Gerald Griffin, author of *The Collegians*, came, along with his brother, in person to Sloperton to urge its acceptance.

Moore was not prepared for the visit, but welcomed his guests. Part of Gerald Griffin's account may be cited as showing an exceedingly able young Irishman's attitude of mind towards the poet (*the* poet), and the impression which Moore left on him:—

> "Oh, my dear L——, I saw the poet! and I spoke to him and he spoke to me, and it was not to bid me 'get out of his way,' as the King of France did to the man who boasted that his majesty had spoken to him; but it was to shake hands with me and to ask me 'How I did, Mr. Griffin?' and to speak of 'my fame.' *My* fame! Tom Moore talk of my fame! Ah the rogue, he was humbugging, L——, I'm afraid. He knew the soft side of an author's heart, and perhaps he had pity on my long, melancholy-looking figure, and said to himself, 'I will make this poor fellow feel pleasant if I can,' for which, with all his roguery, who could help liking and being grateful to him?...

> ..."We found our hero in his study, a table before him, covered with books and papers, a draw half opened and stuffed with letters, a piano also open at a little distance; and the thief himself, a little man, but full of spirits, with eyes,

hands, feet, and frame for ever in motion, looking as if it
would be a feat for him to sit for three minutes quiet in his
chair. I am no great observer of proportions, but he seemed
to me to be a neat-made little fellow, tidily buttoned up,
young as fifteen at heart, though with hair that reminded me
of 'Alps in the sunset'; not handsome perhaps, but
something in the whole cut of him that pleased me; finished
as an actor, but without an actor's affectation; easy as a
gentleman, but without *some* gentlemen's formality; in a
word, as people say when they find their brains begin to run
aground at the fag-end of a magnificent period, we found
him a hospitable, warm-hearted Irishman, as pleasant as
could be himself, and disposed to make others so."

Nothing but civilities resulted from the interview. We learn from Moore's
Diary that he gave them dinner, and told them his opinion of Repeal—which
was, that separation must be considered as its inevitable consequence. This
startled his guests, and they disclaimed "all thoughts and apprehensions" of
such a result. "What strange short-sightedness!" Moore exclaims. It may be
noted that Moore was always exaggerated in his estimate of consequences,
and foretold the most prodigious upheavals as a result of the Reform Bill. It
is also to be noted, that in his opinion, "so hopeless appeared the fate of
Ireland under English government, whether of Whigs or Tories," that he
"would be almost inclined to run the risk of Repeal even with separation as
its too certain consequence, being convinced that Ireland must go through
some violent and convulsive process before the anomalies of her present
position can be got rid of, and thinking such riddance well worth the price,
however dreadful would be the pain of it." So far was Moore from thinking
that Catholic Emancipation settled Ireland's claims in full.

His refusal to represent an Irish constituency was however definitely
conveyed to the envoys in a letter, written for publication, which after
grateful acknowledgment of the honour done him, and of the kindness which
had proposed a national subscription to provide him with the necessary
qualification, ended as follows:—

"Were I obliged to choose which should be my direct
paymaster, the government or the people, I should say
without hesitation, the people; but I prefer holding on my
free course, humble as it is, unpurchased by either; nor shall
I the less continue, as far as my limited sphere of action
extends, to devote such powers as God has gifted me with
to that cause which has always been uppermost in my heart,
which was my first inspiration, and shall be my last—the
cause of Irish freedom."

Moore's friends with one accord congratulated him not only on the taste of his letter, but on his decision. And indeed, quite apart from considerations of money, his position in Parliament would have been impossible. In agreement neither with Whigs nor Tories, he was hardly more in sympathy with O'Connell's party; and he gave strong expression to his feelings in a remarkable lyric included in the tenth and last number of the *Irish Melodies*, published in 1834:—

"The dream of those days when first I sung thee is o'er,
Thy triumph hath stain'd the charm thy sorrows then wore;
And ev'n of the light which Hope once shed o'er thy chains,
Alas, not a gleam to grace thy freedom remains.

"Say, is it that slavery sunk so deep in thy heart,
That still the dark brand is there, though chainless thou art;
And Freedom's sweet fruit, for which thy spirit long burn'd,
Now, reaching at last thy lip, to ashes hath turn'd.

"Up Liberty's steep by Truth and Eloquence led,
With eyes on her temple fix'd, how proud was thy tread!
Ah, better thou ne'er hadst lived that summit to gain,
Or died in the porch, than thus dishonour the fane."

A footnote pointed the meaning in these words.

> "Written in one of those moods of hopelessness and disgust which come occasionally over the mind, in contemplating the present state of Irish patriotism."

Not unnaturally, O'Connell was angry, and his friend Con Lyne wrote to Moore, entreating "an alleviating word." Moore replied, the Journal notes—

> "that I was not surprised at O'Connell's feeling those verses, as I had felt them deeply myself in writing them; but that they were wrung from me by a desire to put on record (in the only work of mine likely to reach after-times) that though going along, heart and soul, with the great cause of Ireland, I by no means went with the spirit or the manner in which that cause had been for a long time conducted."

He admitted that, though the verses were addressed to Ireland, O'Connell had a right to take them to himself, "as he is and has been for a long time, to all public intents and purposes, Ireland." That was just what Moore complained of. He disliked the removal of "all independent and really public-spirited co-operators"; he regarded the position of this "mighty unit of a legion of ciphers" as a threat to freedom, certain to lead to an abuse of power. "Against such abuse of power, let it be placed in what hands it might," he "had all his life revolted and would to the last revolt." From the dignity of this really serious criticism he detracted somewhat by adding that O'Connell's resolution against duelling had done much "to lower the once high tone of feeling in Ireland"; for he omitted to make the necessary observation that, when O'Connell forswore duelling, he by no means forswore personal vituperation. The letter contained no allusion to a feeling which certainly was in Moore's mind when he wrote the verses—namely, his dislike of the "annual stipend from the begging-box." But even without this, it was an explanation ill calculated to alleviate, and Moore thought that public feeling in Ireland might probably run strong against him.

Ireland, however, was constant to her poet. In the next summer (1835) he crossed to Dublin, when the British Association was meeting there, and the demonstration when he was first seen in the theatre went beyond all customary bounds and was not to be checked without a brief speech from the box. But a more ceremonious ovation was to come. Moore decided to go to Wexford to visit the home of his grand-parents, and he was to be the guest of a Mr. Boyse who lived at Bannow. On the approach to this town from Wexford—where Moore was met by his host—the party was encountered by a cavalcade bearing green banners, and so escorted formally to a series of triumphal arches, where a decorated car awaited the poet, with Nine Muses ("some of them remarkably pretty girls") ready to place a crown on his head. It had been arranged that the Muses should follow on foot; but as the crowd pressed in, Moore made three of them get up on the car. As they proceeded slowly along, with a band playing Irish melodies, and the tune set to Byron's "Here's a health to thee, Tom Moore," the hero turned to the pretty Muse behind him and said, "This is a long journey for you." "'Oh, sir,' she exclaimed, with a sweetness and kindness of look not to be found in more artificial life, 'I wish it was more than three hundred miles.'"

Speeches followed, with dancing in the evening, and a green balloon floated over the dancers, bearing to the skies, "Welcome, Tom Moore." That evening there came an express from the Lady Superior of the Presentation Convent at Wexford, begging for a visit to her community. Thither accordingly Moore was taken next day, and, for a crowning ceremony, planted with his own hands—"Oh Cupid, prince of gods and men!"—a myrtle in the convent garden. No sooner was the plant in the earth, than the gardener proclaimed, while filling up the hole, "This will not be called *myrtle* any longer, but the *Star of Airin!*" Well may Moore ask, "Where is the English gardener chat would have been capable of such a flight?"

Demonstrations of this organised character did not recur; but the spontaneous outbursts of feeling manifested themselves, publicly and privately, in ways often a little ridiculous, but not less often really touching. When Moore next visited Ireland (in 1838) he went to the theatre evidently with the purpose of making a speech, and the opportunity was furnished with éclat: "There exists no title of honour or distinction," he told them, "to which I could attach half so much value as that of being called your poet—the poet of the people of Ireland." Certainly the title was not grudged; and the people of Ireland claimed a sort of proprietary right in their bard, as he found when he embarked at Kingstown for his return.

> "The packet was full of people coming to see friends off, and amongst others was a party of ladies, who, I should think, had dined on board, and who, on my being made known to them, almost devoured me with kindness, and at length proceeded so far as to insist on, each of them, *kissing* me. At this time I was beginning to feel the first rudiments of coming *sickness*, and the effort to respond to all this enthusiasm, in such a state of stomach, was not a little awkward and trying. However, I kissed the whole party (about five, I think) in succession, two or three of them being, for my comfort, young and good-looking, and was most glad to get away from them to my berth, which through the kindness of the captain (Emerson) was in his own cabin. But I had hardly shut the door, feeling very qualmish, and most glad to have got over this osculatory operation, when there came a gentle tap at the door, and an elderly lady made her appearance, who said that having heard of all that had been going on, she could not rest easy without being also kissed as well as the rest. So, in the most respectful manner possible, I complied with the lady's request, and then betook myself with a heaving stomach to my berth."

A more modest and less embarrassing act of homage was brought to Moore's notice in London by Panizzi. Among the labourers at work on the buildings of the British Museum was a poor Irishman, who, learning that Moore was sometimes to be seen there, offered a pot of ale to any one who would point him out. Accordingly, next time Moore came, the Irishman was taken to where he could get a sight of the poet, as he sat reading. Such was his pleasure at being able to say "I have seen," that he doubled the pot of ale to his conductor. Again, in 1842 Moore was coming away from a public dinner with Washington Irving, and they found rain falling and themselves in sore need of cab or umbrella.

> "As we were provided with neither," Moore writes, "our plight was becoming serious, when a common cad ran up

to me and said: 'Shall I get you a cab, Mr. Moore? Sure, ain't *I* the man that patronises your Melodies?' He then ran off in search of a vehicle, while Irving and I stood close up, like a pair of male Caryatides under the very narrow projection of a hall door-ledge, and thought at last that we were quite forgotten by my patron. But he came faithfully back, and while putting me into the cab (without minding at all the trifle that I gave him for his trouble) he said confidentially in my ear: 'Now mind, whenever you want a cab, Misthur Moore, just call for Tim Flaherty, I'm your man.' Now this I call *fame*, and of somewhat a more agreeable kind than that of Dante, when the women in the street found him out by the marks of hellfire on his beard."

Green balloons, effusive elderly spinsters and the rest, all had their ridiculous side, and Moore was not slow to see it. But, taking these merely as symptoms of a very genuine affection, one may conclude that he had a fair right to feel in his country's gratitude a deep source of strength and consolation. For the rest, the pleasures of friendship and of society never failed him so long as he was able to enjoy them; and his English friends, in the time when he most needed it, did him a real service.

We have seen that he neither liked the measures of the Whig administration—which included two of his intimates, Lord Lansdowne and Lord John Russell, with many others of his friends—nor was in the least disposed to conceal his dislike of them. Lord John wrote to say that he was glad of Moore's decision not to enter Parliament, as it would pain him to find his friend going into the opposite lobby. But he was none the less inclined to serve Moore, and his first step showed an extreme anxiety to propitiate the poet's easily alarmed scruples. He approached Lord Melbourne, then Premier, with a proposal to bestow a pension on Moore's sons. Melbourne replied, with great justice, that to make a small provision for young men was only an encouragement to idleness, and that whatever was done, should be done for Moore himself. When the administration was reconstructed in July 1835, Lord John offered his friend a place in the State Paper Office, which was declined, and Lord Lansdowne then wrote, approving this refusal, but urging in the strongest terms Moore's acceptance of a pension, "which," he said, "no human being can blame the government for giving or you for accepting. The administration is one of a more popular character as respects your Irish opinions than any which has existed or is likely to exist; and your literary reputation is so established that there is not a country under the sun where literary rewards or distinctions exist in which you would not be recognised as the first and most deserving object of them."

To this Moore replied that he would trust himself entirely to Lord Lansdowne's guidance, and accordingly a letter reached him in Dublin, saying that a pension of £300 a year had been granted him—the first granted by the Administration. On his return from the festivities in Bannow, a letter from Bessy awaited him, which is copied in the Journal:—

> "My dearest Tom,—Can it *really* be true that you have a pension of £300 a year? Mrs., Mr., two Misses and young Longman were here to-day, and tell me it is really the case, and that they have seen it in two papers. Should it turn out true, I know not how we can be thankful enough to those who gave it, or to a Higher Power. The Longmans were very kind and nice and so was *I*, and I invited them *all five* to come at some future time. At present I can think of nothing but £300 a year, and dear Russell jumps and claps his hands for joy.... If the story is true of the £300, pray give dear Ellen £20, and *insist* on her drinking £5 worth of wine *yearly* to be paid out of the £300 a year.... Is it true? I am in a fear of hope and anxiety and feel very oddly. No one to talk to but sweet Buss, who says, 'Now, Papa will not have to work so hard, and will be able to go out a little.' ... N.B.—If this good news be true, it will make a great difference in my *eating*. I shall then indulge in butter to potatoes. *Mind* you do not tell this piece of gluttony to *any* one."

It is pleasant to think of this climax to all the exultation of the Wexford processions. Moore was entitled to say to himself that he had done yeoman's service to the principles for which a Whig administration then stood, and yet had shown his complete independence of persons. What he received, no man could say had been gained by any compromise with his convictions; and it came at a time when it was much needed, for his power of literary production had largely spent itself. The comic inspiration had not indeed wholly run dry, for in 1835 Moore published *The Fudges in England* (a work even more unworthy of its predecessor than most sequels); and in 1836 he entered into an agreement to supply the *Morning Chronicle* with squibs—his *Times* connection having long dropped. But except for this, and the furbishing up in 1839 of *Alciphron*, his first draft in verse of the Egyptian story, nothing more appears to have been produced by him, except the volumes of his *History of Ireland*, which appeared respectively in 1835, 1836, 1840, and 1846.

In fact, within the last seventeen years of his existence, Moore wrote little or nothing but these volumes of history, for which he appears to have received £500 apiece. It will be seen how timely was the succour of the pension.

One other resource, however, and a considerable one, was afforded by a project on which Moore's heart had long been set, and which finally matured in 1837—that of collecting his poetical works into a complete edition. The copyrights of his early Poems had returned to him, but the great bulk of his lyrics was held by Power's widow—for the little publisher had died in 1836, not before disputed accounts had altered the long and friendly relation between him and the author of the *Irish Melodies*. Longmans now bought out her rights for £1000, and paid Moore another thousand for the task of collecting and arranging the poems and writing prefaces, many of which contain interesting biographic detail. It was a long labour, but the edition was finally completed in 1841. Unhappily in that year, he was in no case to be concerned for its success or failure; the Diary hardly refers to this event, of such importance in a man's literary life. Troubles, which had long been heavy and insistent upon him, then fairly culminated.

In spite of his love and talent for society, Moore was essentially a domestic animal; and, as he advanced in life, his home ties were stronger and stronger. The welfare of his children and their health—for they were all delicate—preoccupied him with a constant and painful anxiety, which was, however, more than compensated by the pleasure which he derived from them as they grew up.

He was indeed no baby-worshipper, and notes profanely after one birth: "Bessy doing marvellously well, and the little fright, as all such young things are, prospering also." The first death in his household, that of an infant girl, Byron's goddaughter, affected him mainly as a cause of grief to his wife; and even when he lost his eldest daughter in 1817, truly and deeply though he sorrowed, it is evident enough that the weight of the blow fell on Bessy rather than on him. He was then the one of the two to take thought for the other; not perhaps that he cared less, but that his temperament was then more natural and healthy.

Eight years later he notes the first symptom of what was doubtless a growing infirmity. About a fortnight after his father's death he spent the evening in Dublin with some old friends, and sang a good deal for them.—"In singing 'There's a song of the Olden Time,' the feeling which I had so long suppressed" (for he had been active in endeavouring to keep up his mother's spirits) "broke out; I was obliged to leave the room, and continued sobbing hysterically on the stairs for several minutes." From this onward, the same proclivity manifested itself at intervals with growing vehemence. After any stress of emotion, the plangent quality of his own voice in singing tended to produce one of these outbursts, when it seemed as if his chest must burst under the strain. Yet he always fought against the weakness, and notes more than once how, after a sudden collapse of this kind, he made an effort, and returned to the piano, laughing at himself, while he rattled off gay songs.

But the wrench which of all others seems to have done most to shatter him, came not long after this first breakdown (which dates from the end of 1826, his forty-seventh year); and it found a man strangely altered from what he had been ten or twelve years earlier. His eldest girl's death had left the second, Anastasia, to inherit a double share of affection, and her chronic delicacy kept her parents continually anxious. At last the beginning of the end came early in 1829, just at the moment when Moore was receiving news that Catholic emancipation was a certainty. "Could I ever have thought," he writes, "that such an event would, under any circumstances, find me indifferent to it? Yet such is almost the case at present." Even when he wrote this, he did not realise the worst; the truth was not forced on him till his wife had been "wasting away on the knowledge of it" for three weeks. We have his detailed account of the last fortnight, during which the parents could do nothing but make their child's last days as happy as they could—spending the evenings together with the girl, playing little games, reading aloud and so forth. His description of the end must be quoted:—

> "Next morning (Sunday 8th) I rose early, and, on approaching the room, heard the dear child's voice as strong, I thought, as usual; but on entering, I saw death plainly in her face. When I asked her how she had slept, she said 'Pretty well,' in her usual courteous manner; but her voice had a sort of hollow and distant softness, not to be described. When I took her hand on leaving her, she said (I thought significantly), 'Good-bye, papa.' I will not attempt to tell what I felt at all this. I went occasionally to listen at the door of the room, but did not go in, as Bessy, knowing what an effect (through my whole future life) such a scene would have on me, implored me not to be present at it.... In about three quarters of an hour or less, she called for me, and I came and took her hand for a few seconds, during which Bessy leaned down her head between the poor dying child and me, that I might not see her countenance. As I left the room, too, agonised as her own mind was, my sweet thoughtful Bessy ran anxiously after me, and, giving me a smelling-bottle, exclaimed, 'For God's sake, don't you get ill.' In about a quarter of an hour afterwards, she came to me, and I saw that all was over. I could no longer restrain myself; the feelings I had been so long suppressing found vent, and a fit of loud violent sobbing seized me, in which I felt as if my chest were coming asunder."

Avoiding, after his habit, the actual sensations of horror, Moore took his wife out for a drive while the funeral was going on. There is no doubt, as I have said already, something unmasculine in all this shrinking from the physical impression, and one may trace something of the luxury of grief in the detailed recital. But the note with which it closes has the true accent of tragedy:—

> "And such is the end of so many years of fondness and of hope; and nothing is left us but the dream (which may God in his mercy realise), that we shall see our pure child again in a world more worthy of her."

Gradually, however, time healed the rawness of the wound, and in June of the same year, a new interest was added to Moore's London visits. His eldest boy, Tom, was installed at the Charterhouse, on a nomination secured through Lord Grey, and from this onward the Diary is full of references to the boy's charming (but idle) ways. Moore records dinners with Master Tom,—"who, bless the dear fellow, was more amusing than any of the *beaux esprits,*"—compliments on his beauty, valued all the more because a likeness was noted to his mother, and, in short, gives every instance of parental fondness. We read less perhaps about the other boy, Lord John Russell's godson and namesake, who entered the same school a year or two later, Sir Robert Peel this time giving the nomination. But of both his boys Moore was mighty fond and proud, and it was a moment of great happiness in his life when, in 1830, he conveyed Bessy and the pair of them to Dublin for a visit to his other home in Abbey Street.

> "My sweet sister Nell, just the same gentle spirit as ever; both in great delight with our boys; and my dear Bess never looked so handsome as she did sitting by my mother, with a face bearing the utmost sweetness and affection, all for my sake. Had a most happy family dinner."

The happiness lasted through the visit of six weeks. It was fifteen years since Bessy Moore had been in Ireland, and then she had not lived in the same house with her husband's folk, who consequently knew her mainly by report. "They have now, however," Moore writes, "had her with them as one of themselves, and the result has been what I never could doubt it would be."

Six months later an urgent summons from his sister prepared him for the severing of the closest and oldest of all ties. But when he reached Dublin he found his mother rallied, and her doctor (Crampton) quoting Mother Hubbard at her. After three or four days her strength was so far restored that he felt able to return. But her parting from her son was that of one taking the last farewell. She told him—and indeed she had good right to—that he had always done his duty, and more than his duty, by her and hers. Twelve months later she died, and the news was announced by letter. The effect upon Moore was not that of shock, but rather of deep and saddening depression, which continued for some days and seemed more to be a bodily indisposition than any mental affliction. "To lose such a mother was," he said, "like a part of one's life going out of one."

There was, however, one consolation for this great loss. Moore's sister, Ellen, became a yearly visitor to the Sloperton household, and was drawn fairly into the home circle. Meanwhile, the enthusiasm of his countrymen, and the good help of the pension, brightened matters; and, as the boys grew up, Moore's pleasure in their society increased steadily.

He had procured, under the most distinguished auspices, their admission to a first-rate school; and, fond as he was, he enforced in some matters a standard of conduct more rigid than usual. He set his face against their taking money from any one but their parents, and expressed righteous indignation when Lord Holland defended to him the practice of tipping. Still more indignant was he when the head master represented to him that the elder boy could get an exhibition worth about £100 a year to take him to college, and that Moore need only add an allowance of £150! It seems, however, that exhortations against extravagance prevailed less than the example of spending money freely, which was set to the young Tom by those with whom his father led him to associate. The younger son, Russell, was steadier in character, but decided, like his brother, for the army; and Moore was accordingly put to the heavy expense of outfitting both and launching them in this costly profession. Once launched, however, he was sanguine enough to expect that they could live on their pay.

Tom was gazetted to the 22nd regiment in 1837, and was given six months to study French in Paris, where his father established him under pleasant conditions. Having joined his regiment in 1838 at Cork, he was shortly transferred to Dublin, and here his presence was a pleasure to his aunt, Moore's favourite sister; the news of this made a happy break in the anxieties at Sloperton, where Bessy Moore, always delicate, had just come through a severe illness. In the summer, Moore joined his son and his sister, and was, as we have seen, enormously applauded by his countrymen at the theatre. Next day the father and son were to have dined with Lord Morpeth, the Irish Chief Secretary, but by one of the lapses of memory which began to be habitual with Moore, they presented themselves instead at the Vice-Regal Lodge and were half through dinner before the guest realised what he had done, only to be overwhelmed with expressions of delight at the mistake. It was no doubt a little difficult for a young man with a father who was on such terms with both the people and the rulers of Ireland to realise that he was only the son of a needy and struggling worker, always at straits to make ends meet: and probably Tom himself took the view, expressed to Moore by a friend newly come from Ireland, that such an allowance should be made to the young soldier as would enable him to "live like a gentleman." Moore was angry, and it is easy to sympathise with his disappointment; easy also to condemn his want of foresight.

Tom's regiment was ordered to India, and to India also went the younger son, Russell, for whom a cadetship in the Company's Army had been secured. The younger boy sailed in April 1840, and, although the parting was a heartbreak (above all to the mother), Moore felt at every turn what he calls gratefully "the value of a friendly fame like mine." Directors of the Company, officers aboard ship, governors of provinces, all vied with one another in services; and when the lad reached Calcutta, Lord Auckland, then Governor-General, gave him a room in Government House.

Little good came of all these good offices. Lord Auckland's sincere kindness could only manifest itself in looking after an invalid and writing cordial letters to the parents. Russell Moore's health was quite unequal to the profession he had chosen, and eighteen months after he had reached India, news came that he had been dangerously ill and was ordered home.

In the meanwhile the other son, though keeping his health, was incurring debts. There is a note from Bessy, copied into the Diary, surely as heartbroken a cry as could come from a wife and mother. Enclosing a bill for £120 drawn by Tom upon his father, she writes that she can hardly bring herself to send it:—

> "It has caused me tears and sad thoughts, but to *you* it will bring these and hard *hard* work. Why do people sigh for children? They know not what sorrow will come with them. How *can* you arrange for the payment? and what could have caused him to require such a sum? Take care of yourself; and if you write to him, for God's sake, let him know that it is the very last sum you will or *can* pay for him. My heart is sick when I think of you, and the fatigue of mind and body you are always kept in. Let me know how you think you can arrange this."

A second draft for £100 followed quick on it, and early in the next year, still worse news. The young man had sold his commission and was on his way home. £1500 in all had been spent in fitting him out and purchasing, first an ensigncy, then a lieutenancy; and this was the upshot of so much anxiety and outlay. And the second boy, who had done all that could be hoped of him, was on his way home too, to a sad meeting. "It seemed all but death," Moore writes, "when he stepped out of the carriage exhausted with the journey, and wasted with lung disease." There was a rally for a few months, during which Moore was busy trying to shape some new future for the prodigal Tom, who was remaining in France. Four hundred pounds would have preserved his lieutenancy (being the money actually paid down out of the price of his commission), but Moore refused to find it. He was already reduced to borrowing from a friend, Mr. Boyse, his Wexford host; and though Rogers, Lord Lansdowne, and probably many others would, as Lord John Russell regretfully comments, have willingly advanced the larger sum, they heard nothing of the need. Moore's own object was to secure his son a commission in the Austrian service, but Tom himself wrote from France suggesting the Légion Étrangère. Interest was quickly made with Soult through Madame Adelaide, who received the prodigal and made much of him for his father's sake—"a continuation of that spoiling process," Moore writes sadly, "to which poor Tom (as my son) has been from his childhood subjected." The thing was settled accordingly, not without another draft for a hundred and odd pounds to enable the son to leave for Algiers. A few days before he set out for the new dangers and hardships of Africa, his brother had died peacefully at home. It was only the last straw in a load of trouble that the one remaining child could not even get leave for a farewell visit home, before he launched, under no good omens, into a new career and clime.

The record of the nest year (1843) is short and uninteresting—notes of engagements for the most part. One is characteristic enough to quote:—

> "*March* 23. Breakfasted at Rogers's to meet Jeffrey and Lord John—two of the men I like best among my numerous friends. Jeffrey's volubility (which was always superabundant) becomes even more copious, I think, as he grows older. But I am ashamed of myself for finding any fault with him."

"Lenior et melior fit accedente senecta" is a phrase that has full application to this veteran of letters. The year closed with a cruel hoax (the crueller as it coincided with fresh demands from Tom). Some one in Ireland wrote to inform Moore that £300 had been left him as a testimony of regard. Moore had suspicions, but he adds:—

> "There was an air of truth and reality which half lured my poor Bess and myself into hailing it as a providential God-send. Already, indeed, her generous heart was apportioning out the different presents it would enable her to make to my sister, to the poor H——s, etc. Alas! alas! I wish no worse to the ingenious gentleman who penned the letter than an exactly similar disappointment."

I shall add the next entry in the Diary, Moore's farewell to the year 1843:—

> "A strange life mine; but the best as well as pleasantest part of it lies *at home*. I told my dear Bessy, this morning, that

while I stood at my study window, looking out at her, as she crossed the field, I sent a blessing after her. 'Thank you, bird,' she replied, 'that's better than money'; and so it is. Bird is a pet name she gave me in our younger days, and was suggested by Hamlet's words, 'Hillo, ho, ho, boy! come, bird, come'; being the call, it seems, which falconers use to their hawk in the air, when they would have him come down to them."

What one feels on reading these passages, and contrasting them with many earlier ones, is perhaps best expressed by assenting to the view of Miss Berry, recorded in the Diary. Moore had taken the liberty of an old friend in going unasked to one of her famous *soirées*, and on his saying something of this:—

"She reverted in her odd way to the early days of our acquaintance, and said, 'I didn't so much like you in those days. You were too-too—what shall I say?' 'Too brisk and airy perhaps,' said I. 'Yes,' she replied, taking hold of one of my grizzly locks, 'I like you better since you have got these.' I could then overhear her, after I left her, say to the person with whom I had found her speaking, 'That's as good a creature as ever lived!'"

The light and buoyant nature, which had been so sorely battered, received its final shock soon after the date to which I have brought this story. 1844 was spent in scriving over the *History*,—Moore repelling now the friendly advances even of his Bowood neighbours, yet with difficulty repelling them. The task was finished at last in the spring of 1845, but there remained the need of a preface, and Moore records that after various endeavours he left this, "in utter despair," to the publishers to provide. Later in the year, the annual visit from his sister Ellen made a brightness in the house, now so quiet; and after she had gone, there came letters from Tom asking for money for a trip home. It was sent, and he wrote back rejoicing at the prospect, but explaining that he should not come before spring owing to a cough which he had contracted. The words were ominous, and both his parents almost made up their minds that they were never to see him again.

The foreboding was only too well justified. But the first blow which fell was one little looked for. Ellen Moore died suddenly in her bed. A month later came from Africa "a strange and ominous-looking letter which we opened with trembling hands, and it told us that my son Tom was dead." I add one last quotation from the Diary.

"The last of our five children now are gone and I am left desolate and alone. Not a single relative have I now left in the world."

That is practically the end of Moore's life. A severe illness followed, and "when he recovered," says Lord John Russell, "he was a different man." "Nothing seemed to rest upon his mind," and, with his memory, his wit had gone also. He made an excursion to town in 1846 to superintend the production of the last volume of his history, and one year later still, to be the guest of Rogers, who was to Moore, at any rate, a most considerate, loyal, helpful, and constant friend. But what he wrote to this friend from Sloperton was true: "I am sinking here into a mere vegetable." So, peacefully at the last, after five years of mere breathing, in which neither joy nor sorrow touched him, he faded out of life; watched over to the last by the woman who had grown more necessary to him with every year.

He left her unprovided with money, yet not without provision. The Memoirs which he, himself a great lover and reader of such literature, had scrupulously kept for a period of close on thirty years, were always designed to be a posthumous resource; and he had confided them by a will made many years earlier to the care of Lord John Russell. Had he foreseen that the friend of whom he asked this office would be charged with the cares of an Administration, when it fell to be accomplished, the request would probably not have been made; but being made, it was duly honoured, and Moore, who had always liked impressive auspices for his children at the font,[1] had himself a Prime Minister for his biographer.

The work might perhaps have been better done by a man less fully occupied, but the purpose for which the Memoirs were written could not have been more fully served. The Longmans offered £3000 for the Memoirs, if Lord John would edit them, and it was found that for this sum an annuity could be bought, equal to the pension which had for the last part of Moore's life been the sole resource of the household. Bessy Moore lived and died in Sloperton, and was laid in the churchyard beside her husband and her children; and old men in the little Wiltshire hamlet remember her and her good works—the only one of her lifelong pleasures and occupations which was left to this good woman, whom it is impossible to think of as lonely. The record of her life and her husband's—for the two are inseparable—may close with as touching a little attention as was ever paid by an elderly man to his elderly wife. In 1839, when money was no way plenty with him, Moore sent five pounds to a friend, which the friend was to forward anonymously to Bessy for her poor—thus giving her the pleasure which he judged she would most value, without the distress of thinking that he must labour more to make up the little outlay.

[1] Lady Donegal, Byron, Lord Lansdowne, Lord John Russell, and Dr. Parr were among the sponsors.

CHAPTER VII
GENERAL APPRECIATION

Of Moore's personal qualities not much remains to be said; but we may endeavour to account for the fact that he became the fashion when he was one-and-twenty, and retained an undiminished vogue for a matter of forty years.

His singing undoubtedly first brought him into notice; a late passage in the Journal recalls, across a gulf of years, one evening at a musical assembly, when people laughed and stared to see a little Irish lad brought out to sing after some distinguished professionals; and how the contemptuous wonder was changed to wonder of a very different kind when the singer had produced his effect. Hard upon these successes, and helped by them to succeed, came his *Anacreon*, a volume of easy, springing and melodious verse, flushed with prodigal youth; and the combination of the two gifts excited such widespread admiration, that their fortunate possessor was much sought out. In these early days Moore was no doubt largely what is called a ladies' man, and the genius for friendship which he possessed showed itself a good deal with women. From these years dates the long intimacy with Lady Donegal and her sister, Miss Godfrey—an intimacy which his marriage in no way ended. These friends continued for years to correspond with him and to advise on his affairs. But after marriage, he formed no new friendships with women. His delight in feminine society never left him, but it was of a special order.

Moore was by universal consent the very best of company; a talker who delighted in the give and take of conversation, and was at least as well pleased with other people's wit as his own. He had perhaps the less occasion to be jealous, having in his singing a resource which made him unrivalled. This talent, however, he would only use in a mixed company—"hating this operation with he-hearers," as he notes somewhere of a men's dinner when he was forced to depart from his habit. To women and for them he sung, while his singing powers lasted; but it is not unfair to say that he valued women in society chiefly as decorative accessories and as an audience. Among the innumerable good things noted in his Diary, hardly one is credited to a woman. And, well as he liked singing to a mixed audience, it is clear that his chief pleasure, as he advanced in life, lay in the society of men.

With men, his intimacies were numerous enough, for Moore was as popular in clubs as in drawing-rooms, and most of his intimates were persons of title. Byron said that "Tommy dearly loved a lord"; and a hundred people know this saying, for one who has seen Byron's sincerer utterance (not published in Moore's edition of the *Life and Letters*):—"I have had the kindest letter from Moore. I do think that man is the best-hearted—the only *hearted* being I ever encountered; and his talents are equal to his feelings." It is therefore worth while to note that Moore by no means loved any or every lord. He did, however, certainly desire to associate with those who possessed hereditary station and had the brains to make a generous use of it, both in acquiring power and in drawing to their houses men like Moore himself—or Sydney Smith, whom Moore loved better to meet than any lord, except perhaps Lord John Russell. His deliberate opinion, stated more than once in the Diary, was that in his time the most agreeable and also the purest tone of society was to be found at the top of the social ladder. And in point of fact he was admitted to intimacy with the Whig aristocracy in its most brilliant day. Bowood and Holland House, as Moore knew them, were probably the best things of their kind that England has ever seen.

For a description of the charm which made him not only welcome but courted in these great houses, it would be hard to better that set down by Haydon the painter, in his autobiography:—

> "Met Moore at dinner, and spent a very pleasant three hours. He told his stories with a hit-or-miss air, as if accustomed to people of rapid apprehension. It being asked at Paris who they would have as godfather for Rothschild's child, 'Talleyrand,' said a Frenchman. *'Pourquoi, Monsieur?' 'Parce qu'il est le moins chrétien possible.'* Moore is a delightful, gay, voluptuous, refined, natural creature; infinitely more unaffected than Wordsworth; not blunt and uncultivated like Chantrey, or bilious and shivering like Campbell. No affectation, but a true, refined, delicate, frank poet, with sufficient air of the world to prove his fashion, sufficient honesty of manner to show fashion has not corrupted his native taste; making allowance for prejudices instead of condemning them, by which he seemed to have none himself; never talking of his own work from an intense consciousness that everybody else did; while Wordsworth is talking of his own productions from apprehension that they are not enough matter of conversation. Men must not be judged too hardly. Success or failure will either destroy or better the finest natural parts. Unless one had heard Moore tell the above story of Talleyrand, it would have been impossible to conceive the air of half-suppressed impudence, the delicate light-horse canter of phrase, with which the words floated out of his sparkling anacreontic mouth."

To the personal notability which his social talent secured him, Moore owed much of his later successes as a prose writer: in part because of the access which it afforded to sources of information; in part because everybody knew him, and read with expectation whatever he wrote. But as a poet, his fame was a thing wholly independent of personal charm. People knew that the writer whose songs they had by heart was courted in the most brilliant world; they knew also that he had shown in various difficult junctures a high spirit of honour and independence. But they knew these things mainly because they liked his poetry. Prom all this contemporary fame of the poet, one must try to analyse what remains.

Moore himself—except during his stay in Paris, when much adulation led him to question whether he might not perhaps really deserve to rank with Scott and Byron—always regarded his poetry as unlikely to last. His modesty was real; for not only did he feel himself overshadowed by Scott and Byron, but, placed in the difficult position of knowing himself popular and Wordsworth all but unread, he never hesitated in recognising Wordsworth's as by far the greater talent. His growing admiration for this poet is all the more remarkable, because at many meetings his sense of ridicule was frequently stimulated by Wordsworth's egotism and "soliloquacious" habit of conversation. Coleridge he could neither like nor understand, and it seems that he did not care much for Shelley. But throughout his Diary, one finds him manifesting, in many passages, the conviction that these men, the unread, were better artists than himself; and he notes with exceptional pleasure any word of praise from them, as if he expected only dislike and disapprobation for his facile and popular verses. Not less should it be noted, that none of them praised his longer poems, but all (except of course Wordsworth) spoke with sincere enthusiasm of his lyrics. The opinion of Landor and of Shelley was, in effect, that expressed by Moore himself: that of his whole work the *Irish Melodies* alone were likely to last into future times. But both Shelley (as reported by his wife) and Landor agreed in attributing to Moore's lyrics the highest poetical merit. How far critical opinion may ultimately bear out this estimate must remain to be seen; but probably the depreciation of Moore's work, which prevails at present, is hardly more judicious than Lord John Russell's extravagant over-praise.

The last century has been one of increasing virtuosity in the management of lyric metres. From Cowper and Crabbe to Mr. Swinburne, is a strange distance; and it has not been sufficiently realised that Moore is very largely responsible for the advance. Many critics have noted the change from the strictly syllabic scansion of Pope's school to metres like those of Tennyson's *Maud*, and a hundred later poems, in which syllabic measurement is wholly discarded. It has been noted also that, even in the freer metres of the sixteenth and seventeenth centuries, lyric writers confined themselves to variations of the trochee or iambic, and that an anapæstic or dactylic measure is hardly found before Waller. But it has hardly been recognised that till Moore began to use these triple feet, no poet used them with dexterity and confidence.

Coleridge, it is true, and Scott had employed a broken rhythm, substituting the temporal for the syllabic ictus, to vary the monotony of the eight-syllabled narrative verse. But, to judge of the best that could be done before Moore's time with a purely anapæstic measure, one may refer to Wordsworth's "At the corner of Wood Street, when daylight appears." These verses are sufficiently destitute of the lyrical quality which is so constantly present in any work of Shelley's. But Moore had done all but all his best work, before Shelley had written six poems worthy of remembrance.

Going back, as we have seen, to the seventeenth century for his inspiration in style, Moore began by using only the trochaic and iambic measures. In the *Epistles and Odes*, we find one epistle (that to Atkinson) written in well-managed anapæsts, but more notable is the very delicate rhythm of the Canadian Boat Song—inspired by a tune. It is Moore's great distinction that he brought into English verse something of the variety and multiplicity of musical rhythms. When the *Irish Melodies* began to appear, it is no wonder that readers should have been dazzled by the skill with which a profusion of metres were handled; and the poet showed himself even more inventive in rhythms than in stanzas.

The most curious part of the matter is that Moore was really importing into English poetry some of the characteristics of a literature which he did not know. He had not a word of Gaelic, and (like O'Connell) desired to see it die out. He observes that Spanish alone of European metrical systems employs "assonantic" instead of consonantic rhyme, though he was bred in a country where rhyme of this order had been brought to an extraordinary pitch of perfection. But he based his work upon Irish times, composed in the primitive manner, before music was divorced from poetry. One may say, virtually, that in fitting words to these tunes, he reproduced in English the rhythms of Irish folk song.

The thing was not done completely: for instance, in the first number of the *Melodies*, the song "Erin, the smile and the tear in thine eye," is to the tune of "Eileen Aroon," and the Irish words (which survive in this instance and, I am told by my friend Mr. O'Neil Russell, in only one other), do not correspond in metre with Moore's. He has varied the tune, and is consequently using a different stanza, which corresponds with the Irish only in the last three lines of the refrain. In the other instance, that of "O blame not the bard," there is a general correspondence in metre, but here the Irish metre is one not very different from an ordinary English stanza—though, as usual in Irish folk-poetry, the line is measured by time and not by syllables.

The need for fitting metre to music forced Moore into employing a wide variety of stanzas; and his example was of service in a day which had been little used to anything but the couplet and quatrain of three or four well-worn types. But by far more remarkable was the achievement in three separate poems of a metrical effect wholly new in English. Of these, one is probably the most beautiful lyric that Moore ever wrote:—

"At the mid hour of night, when the stars are weeping, I fly
To the lone vale we loved, when life shone warm in thine eye;
And I think oft, if spirits can steal from the regions of air,
To revisit past scenes of delight, thou wilt come to me there,
And tell me our love is remember'd, even in the sky!

"Then I sing the wild song 'twas once such pleasure, to hear,
When our voices, commingling, breathed, like one, on the ear;
And, as Echo far off through the vale my sad orison rolls,
I think, O my love! 'tis thy voice, from the Kingdom of Souls,
Faintly answering still the notes that once were so dear."

In the second, the same structure is used for the line, but with a different and simpler stanza:—

"Through grief and through danger thy smile hath cheer'd my way,
Till hope seemed to bud from each thorn that round me lay;
The darker our fortune, the brighter our pure love burn'd;
Till shame into glory, till fear into zeal was turn'd;
Yes, slave as I was, in thy arms my spirit felt free,
And bless'd even the sorrows that made me more dear to thee.

"Thy rival was honour'd, whilst thou wert wrong'd and scorn'd,
Thy crown was of briers, while gold her brows adorn'd;
She woo'd me to temples, while thou layest hid in caves,
Her friends were all masters, while thine, alas! were slaves;
Yet cold in the earth, at thy feet, I would rather be,
Than wed what I love not, or turn one thought from thee.

"They slander thee sorely, who say thy vows are frail—
Hadst thou been a false one, thy cheek had look'd less pale,
They say too, so long thou hast worn those lingering chains,
That deep in thy heart they have printed their servile stains—
Oh! foul is the slander—no chain could that soul subdue—
Where shineth *thy* spirit, there liberty shineth too!"

In these verses we have of course an allegory. By a fashion common in Irish poetry, the poet expresses as a love song his political allegiance—though here the Catholic Church, rather than Ireland, is the "Dark Rosaleen" or "Kathleen ni Houlihan," to whom the passion is addressed. The third of this remarkable group has been quoted already: it is Moore's rebuke to Ireland, or to O'Connell, "The dream of those days when first I sung thee is o'er"; and it is very notable that for such an occasion he should have chosen his most distinctively Irish manner. The peculiarity of these metres—the dragging, wavering cadence that half baulks the ear—is the distinctive characteristic of Irish verse. No English poet, so far as I know, has caught it; but Mangan gave this character to some of his finest renderings from the Irish, and in our own day Mr. Yeats has shown an increasing tendency towards this subtle and evasive beauty.

It is I think mainly as an artist in metre that Moore still holds an importance in the history of English poetry; and any one considering the poems just quoted will see how individual and original were his achievements. But the admirable qualities in his verse by which he impressed his contemporaries were rather those of lightness and swiftness: its sweetness, of which much was made, is a good deal less admirable. For this, however, the nature of his best lyric work was largely responsible.

He wrote songs to be sung; and the best verse is not that which sings best. Language has to be softened down for singing, as it need not be for speech; and this softening approaches to emasculation. The habit of writing for music injured Moore's versification even when he wrote narrative verse; and we have the result in the excessive smoothness of *Lalla Rookh*.

Even more unfortunately did the medium of production affect his style. Moore's conception of singing was certainly not one in which the words were to be sacrificed to the music; but he wrote his words to be sung; and words for singing must carry their meaning easily through the ear to the intelligence—for what is sung can never be caught so easily as what is spoken. He was led, therefore, to use a strict economy of ideas; to expand rather than condense his meaning. Take such a verse as this (from "Farewell, but whenever you welcome the hour"):—

"Let Fate do her worst; there are relics of joy,
Bright dreams of the past, which she cannot destroy,
Which come in the night-time of sorrow and care,
And tiring back the features that joy used to wear.
Long, long be my heart with such memories fill'd!
Like the vase, in which roses have once been distill'd—
You may break, you may shatter the vase if you will,

But the scent of the roses will hang round it still"—

and set beside it Shelley's:—

"Music when soft voices die
Vibrates in the memory:
Odours when sweet violets sicken
Live within the sense they quicken;
Rose leaves when the rose is dead
Are heaped for the beloved's bed;
And so thy thoughts, when thou art gone,
Love itself shall slumber on."

There is no doubt of Shelley's superiority; but on the other hand Shelley's words, if sung, would not carry their sense so easily as Moore's. The mind would lose itself in the quick succession of metaphors; and it is noticeable in the *Melodies* how often the whole song is merely the skilful and deliberate evolution of a single metaphor—an art akin to the rhetorician's. This is true even of the famous "Oh breathe not his name"; and, indeed, it is not less true that Emmet's utterance was the real poem—Moore's only an ingenious amplification of the thought—or rather of a part of it.

One must bear in mind, then, that Moore's lyrics are verse written for public utterance, designed to produce their impression instantly, and not to sink slowly into the mind: and it is useless to compare them with the packed thought of Shakespeare's sonnets, Wordsworth's odes, or whatever else is in the highest category of lyric poetry.

There is, however, a class of verse to which hardly anything can be preferred, and in it are not only the songs of Shakespeare, but some of Scott's and many of Burns's; music as simple as a bird's, dealing in the simplest emotions, free from all taint of rhetoric. In that class I do not think that anything of Moore's can be placed. But one must remember when Moore wrote. He wrote under the influence of the eighteenth century, when the reaction towards a style less coloured by convention had barely set in. He wrote, it is true, when Scott did, and not long after Burns; but both Burns and Scott (whenever Scott is at his best) had the guiding inspiration of a perfect style in the Lowland vernacular poetry, never sophisticated by criticism, or by the intrusion of a dialect of polite prose. And if one compares Moore's lyrics with the best that Burns wrote *in English*, when liable to the influence of Gray and the rest, I do not think it is to Burns that the preference will be given—by the impartial arbiter, who should be neither Scot nor Irish.

It is, however, unreasonable to talk about Moore's lyrics as a whole, for the work falls into two distinct categories, and in one of these Moore must be pronounced the equal of any man who ever lived. The lighter numbers breathe the very spirit of gaiety, united to a real distinction of style:—

"Drink to her, who long
Hath waked the poet's sigh,
The girl who gave to song
What gold could never buy."

Still more characteristic perhaps is another, so melodious and so roguish:—

"The young May moon is beaming, love,
The glow-worm's lamp is gleaming, love,
How sweet to rove
Through Morna's grove,
When the drowsy world is dreaming, love!

Then awake!—the heavens look bright, my dear,
'Tis never too late for delight, my dear,
And the best of all ways
To lengthen our days
Is to steal a few hours from the night, my dear."

Neither Prior nor Praed, nor any other master of the lighter lyric, has equalled these; and better still, perhaps, is the well-known verse:—

"The time I've lost in wooing,
In watching and pursuing
The light that lies
In woman's eyes,
Has been my heart's undoing.
Though Wisdom oft has sought me,
I scorn'd the lore she brought me.
My only books
Were woman's looks,
And folly's all they've taught me."

But it should be noticed that the gay metre, which fits this last humour like a glove, is on the very next page applied to a serious theme, which it dishonours, none the less for the refrain tacked on:—

"Oh, where's the slave so lowly,
Condemn'd to chains unholy,
Who, could he burst
His bonds at first,
Would pine beneath them slowly?
What soul, whose wrongs degrade it,

Would wait till time decay'd it,
When thus its wing
At once may spring
To the throne of Him who made it?
Farewell, Erin,—farewell, all,
Who live to weep our fall."

The tune no doubt demanded the double rhyme, and in Irish, it must be remembered, double rhymes do not involve a jingle, being only an assonance of the vowels ("weepeth" for instance would be a full rhyme to "meeting"). Moore, writing English, was profuse in double rhymes, and did not even shrink from the device, proper only, with few exceptions, to trivial and comic verse, of forming the rhyme with two words. Thus, for instance, we find him destroying a fine opening in the lyric:—

"Avenging and bright fall the swift sword of Erin
On him who the brave sons of Usna betray'd—
For every fond eye he hath waken'd a tear in,
A drop from his heart-wounds shall weep o'er her blade."

All this criticism is of course from the standpoint of a reader. Considered as compositions to be sung, the *Melodies* are probably little injured by this defect in style, and the rhetorical effect of—

"Where's the slave so lowly
Condemned to chains unholy,"

may even gain by the amplitude of the ending.

Throughout, I think, it can hardly be denied that the poetry of Moore's lyrics lies very close to eloquence and is remote from that distinctive quality of the highest poetic expression which transcends rhetoric altogether. A proof lies in the fact that these songs are among the most translatable of all poetry— and among the most translated. Their charm lies, like that of French poetry (before the Romantic movement), in the felicitous expression of an apt or moving thought. It might be difficult to express the idea so well in another language; but no one would feel it impossible. Take such lines as:—

"To-morrow, and to-morrow, and to-morrow,
Creeps in this petty pace from day to day,"

and the most careless will feel that, beyond the idea expressed, there is an accent, and a suggestion as if of gesture, somehow incorporated with the actual words and inseparable from them. An effect of this kind is rarely achieved by Moore. His words always clearly convey the definite thought, but they hardly ever convey anything more. We have, in the most characteristic examples of his art, a quite extraordinary eloquence, in such poems as those on Emmet and on Emmet's betrothed, or that on Lord Edward ("When he who adores thee"), or "The Prince's Song" ("When first I met thee"); or again in the fierce strain of "Sad one of Sion." The last stanzas of this may be quoted; they compare the fate that was Judea's with the fate that may be Ireland's.

"Yet hadst thou thy vengeance—yet came there the morrow,
That shines out, at last, on the longest dark night,
When the sceptre that smote thee with slavery and sorrow,
Was shiver'd at once, like a reed, in thy sight.

"When that cup, which for others the proud Golden City
Had brimm'd full of bitterness, drench'd her own lips;
And the world she had trampled on heard, without pity,
The howl in her halls, and the cry from her ships.

"When the curse Heaven keeps for the haughty came over
Her merchants rapacious, her rulers unjust,
And, a ruin, at last, for the earthworm to cover,
The Lady of Kingdoms lay low in the dust."

Nothing could be more complete and rounded as the expression of an emotion than "The Harp that once"; but I find less rhetoric and even more poetry in the lovely address to the spirit of Irish music which closed the sixth number of the *Melodies*, and should have closed the series. Familiar as it is, Moore has become so far obsolete, for English readers, that it may be given here:—

"Dear Harp of my Country! in darkness I found thee,
The cold chain of silence had hung o'er thee long,
When proudly, my own Island Harp, I unbound thee,
And gave all thy chords to light, freedom, and song!
The warm lay of love and the light note of gladness
Have waken'd thy fondest, thy liveliest thrill;
But so oft hast thou echo'd the deep sigh of sadness,
That even in thy mirth it will steal from thee still.

"Dear Harp of my Country! farewell to thy numbers,
This sweet wreath of song is the last we shall twine!
Go, sleep with the sunshine of Fame on thy slumbers,
Till touch'd by some hand less unworthy than mine:
If the pulse of the patriot, soldier, or lover,
Have throbb'd at our lay, 'tis thy glory alone;

I was but as the wind, passing heedlessly over,
And all the wild sweetness I waked was thy own."

Except in the *Sacred Songs* there is nothing in Moore's work fit to stand beside such lyrics as these; and the finest of these *Songs* breathes an inspiration very like that of the *Melodies*:—

"Fall'n is thy throne, O Israel!
Silence is o'er thy plains;
Thy dwellings all lie desolate,
Thy children weep in chains."

Another opens with a very beautiful verse:—

"The turf shall be my fragrant shrine;
My temple, Lord! that arch of thine;
My censer's breath the mountain airs,
And silent thoughts my only prayers."

But here, in the working out of the idea, one feels, as so often in Moore, rather sated with sweetness. For an extreme example of this cloying ornament, to which he owed so much of his popularity, one would quote:—

"Oh! had we some bright little isle of our own,
In a blue summer ocean far off and alone,
Where a leaf never dies in the still-blooming bowers,
And the bee banquets on through a whole year of flowers;
Where the sun loves to pause
With so fond a delay,
That the night only draws
A thin veil o'er the day;
Where simply to feel that we breathe, that we live,
Is worth the best joy that life elsewhere can give."

There is no flaw in such work, but the taste is too florid. Occasionally, however, we find his taste wholly at fault in the choice of a phrase, as in "Sir Knight, *I feel not the least alarm*," or the still worse "Believe me, if all those *endearing young charms*,"—a lapse into the worst dulcification of confectionery.

There is of course a fashion in verse as in anything else, and Moore's excellences are precisely the least congenial to the current taste in criticism. There is a fashion for nakedness of expression, and Moore always shrank from brutality; there is a fashion for strained uses of language, and Moore was always studiously accurate and lucid. But it may be questioned whether, setting aside the opinion of professed and professional critics, Moore's poetry would not be found to retain a vigorous life. He was never, and never wished to be, in the least esoteric; his object was to be understood by all. A poet who insists upon this aim must perhaps sacrifice something, but he may also achieve something not common. Oddly enough, there is no poet in English except Goldsmith who appeals to simple people so much as Moore. These two can often bring poetry home in triumph where even Shakespeare would never find an entrance.

But Moore's importance in the history of literature lies in his connection not with English but with Irish literature. It was not for nothing that Ireland hailed him for her first national poet. Nowadays, even English readers probably know that poetry of a class not inferior to Moore's was being written in Ireland in Moore's lifetime. He was the younger contemporary of Seaghan Clarach, the full contemporary of Raftery. But the nation which stood behind Grattan—that fused, bi-lingual people welded into a unity during the years that led up to 1782, yet not so closely welded but that a wedge could be driven in—accepted English as the language of political leadership; and it caught eagerly at any manifestation of its national unity. Deprived of a parliament, it found a poet of its own. It heard for the first time in the *Irish Melodies* a song that came from the heart of Ireland, uttered in a language which nine out of every ten Irishmen could understand. A journalist, writing in 1810, says: "Moore has done more for the revival of our national spirit than all the political writers whom Ireland has seen for a century." The other Irishmen who had shown great literary talent—Burke, Goldsmith, and Sheridan—belonged body and soul to English letters. Moore's case was different. Almost without knowing it, he wrote primarily for his own countrymen, and in return they honoured him, not perhaps on this side idolatry, but with a sane instinct, because he had done for Ireland, what neither Seaghan Clarach nor Raftery, nor all the bards of Munster and Connaught, could at that moment do for her. He had given a voice to Ireland; he had put into her mouth a song of her own.

Standing apart now, from the times and circumstances in which Moore wrote, we can see that what Ireland got from him was not all gain. The literature produced so profusely in the days of Young Ireland, and modelled mainly upon him, echoes only too faithfully his declamatory tone; and worse than that, it is flooded by the exuberance of sentiment, which was Moore's besetting weakness. Other models, and, it is to be hoped, better ones, now are rapidly replacing those of Moore and his followers; with the younger generation, even in Ireland, he has lost his hold. But in Ireland his poetry is still, as a matter of course, familiar to all Irishmen of the nationalist persuasion, young and old. And for the older men, he has lost none of his magic. To them such criticism as is found in this book will seem, one must fear, a kind of impiety and certainly of ingratitude; for they remember the days when many and many an Irish peasant, leaving his country for the New World, carried with him two books—*Moore's Melodies* and the *Key of Heaven*.

And certainly it is no small title to fame for a poet that he was in his own country for at least three generations the delight and consolation of the poor. Tattered and thumbed copies of his poems, broadcast through Ireland, represent better his claim to the interest of posterity than whatever comely and autographed editions may be found among the possessions of Bowood and Holland House.

APPENDIX
DATES OF MOORE'S PUBLICATIONS

The kindness of Mr. Andrew Gibson allows me to reprint from a privately circulated pamphlet the following catalogue, compiled by him for his Lecture (delivered in Belfast), on "Thomas Moore and his First Editions"[1]:—

List showing the order in which the various Editions were taken up in the course of Mr. Gibson's Lecture; and giving, together with the sizes, the actual or supposed dates of publication.[2]

Works with music are distinguished by an asterisk.

1. The Odes of Anacreon. 4to. 1800.[3]

2. The Poetical Works of the late Thomas Little, Esq. 8vo. 1801.

3. Sheet Songs*:[4]
(a) Published by F. Rhames, No. 16 Exchange Street, Dublin, before Sir John Stevenson received his knighthood in 1803:—
Buds of Roses, Virgin Flowers, a chearful Glee, for 4 voices, the poetry translated from Anacreon by T. Moore, Esqr. The Music composed (& respectfully dedicated to the Honble. Augustus Barry) by J.A. Stevenson, Mus. D. Price Is. 6d. British.

Though Fate, my Girl, a Canzonet with an Accompaniment for the Piano Forte or Harp, the Poetry by Thos. Moore, Esqr. The Music Composed by J.A. Stevenson, Mus. D. Price 1/1.

Dear! in pity do not speak, a Canzonet for two Voices, with an Accompaniment for the Piano Forte or Harp, the Poetry by Thos. Moore, Esqr., set to Music by J.A. Stevenson, Mus. D. Price 1s.

Scotch Song [Mary, I believ'd thee true] with an Accompaniment for the Piano Forte or Harp, the Poetry by Thos. Moore, Esqr., the Music Composed by J.A. Stevenson, Mus. D.

Price 6d.

(b) Music as well as words by Moore. Published by Carpenter, Old Bond Street, London:—

Oh Lady Fair! A Ballad for Three Voices. Dedicated to the Rt. Honble. Lady Charlotte Rawdon. 1802.

When Time who steals our years away. A Ballad dedicated to Mrs. Henry Tighe of Rosanna.

Fly from the World O Bessy to me.

Farewell Bessy.

Good Night.

Friend of my Soul.

(c) "Dublin, Published by F. Rhames, 16 Exchange Street. Price 3 British Shillings":—

Give me the Harp. A Chorus Glee, with an Accompaniment for two Performers on one Piano Forte. Sung with great applause at the Irish Harmonic Club on Wednesday, the 4th May, 1803, when that Society had the Honor of entertaining His Excellency Earl Hardwicke. The Words translated from Anacreon by Thomas Moore, Esqr. The Music composed by Sir John A. Stevenson, Mus. Doc.

(d) "London, Printed for James Carpenter, Old Bond Street. 1805":—

A Canadian Boat Song [Faintly as tolls the evening chime] Arranged for Three Voices. By Thomas Moore, Esqr.

4. Epistles, Odes, and other Poems. 4to. 1806.

5. Irish Melodies. First Number. Fol. [1808]*.[5]

6. Irish Melodies. Second Number. Fol. [1808]*.

7. Corruption and Intolerance: two Poems. 8vo. 1808.

8. The Sceptic: a Philosophical Satire. 8vo. 1809.[6]

9. Irish Melodies. Third Number. Fol. [1810]*.

10. A Letter to the Roman Catholics of Dublin. 8vo. 1810.

11. A Melologue upon National Music. ?Fol. [1811]*.[7]

12. M.P. or The Blue Stocking. Sm. fol. [1811]*.

13. M.P. or The Blue-Stocking. 8vo. 1811.[8]

14. Irish Melodies. Fourth Number. Fol. [1811]*.[9]

15. Intercepted Letters; or, The Twopenny Postbag. 8vo. 1813.

16. Irish Melodies. Fifth Number. Fol. [1813]*.[10]

17. A Collection of the Vocal Music of Thomas Moore. Sm. fol. [1814]*.

18. Irish Melodies. Sixth Number. Fol. [1815]*.[11]

19. The World at Westminster. A Periodical Publication. 2 vols. 12mo. 1816.

20. Sacred Songs. First Number. Fol. [1816]*.[12]

21. Lalla Rookh. 4to. 1817.

22. The Fudge Family in Paris. 8vo. 1818.

23. National Airs. First Number. Sm. fol. 1818*.[13]

24. Irish Melodies. Seventh Number. Fol. 1818*.[14]

25. Tom Crib's Memorial to Congress. 8vo. 1819.

26. National Airs. Second Number. Sm. fol. 1820*.

27. Irish Melodies, with a Melologue upon National Music. 8vo. 1820.

28. Irish Melodies. Eighth Number. Fol. 1821*.[15]

29. Irish Melodies, by Thomas Moore, Esq. With an Appendix, containing the Original Advertisements and the Prefatory Letter on Music. 8vo. 1821.[16]

30. National Airs. Third Number. Sm. fol. 1822*.

31. National Airs. Fourth Number. Sm. fol. 1822*.

32. The Loves of the Angels, a Poem. 8vo. 1823.

33. The Loves of the Angels, an Eastern Romance. The Fifth Edition. 8vo. 1823.[17]

34. Fables for the Holy Alliance, Rhymes on the Road, etc., etc. 8vo. 1823.

35. Sacred Songs. Second Number. Fol. [1824]*.

36. Irish Melodies. Ninth Number. Fol. [1824]*.

37. Memoirs of Captain Rock. 12mo. 1824.

38. Memoirs of the Life of the Right Honourable Richard Brinsley Sheridan. 4to. 1825.

39. National Airs. Fifth Number. Sm. fol. [1826]*.

40. Evenings in Greece. First Evening. Sm. fol. [1826]*.

41. The Epicurean, a Tale. 12mo. 1827.

42. National Airs. Sixth Number. Sm. fol. [1827]*.

43. A Set of Glees. Sm. fol. [1827]*.

44. Odes upon Cash, Corn, Catholics, and other Matters. 8vo. 1828.

45. Legendary Ballads. Sm. fol. [1830]*.

46. Letters and Journals of Lord Byron: with Notices of his Life. 2 vols., 4to., 1830.[18]

47. The Life and Death of Lord Edward Fitzgerald. 2 vols., 8vo. 1831.

48. The Summer Fête. Sm. fol. [1831]*.

49. Evenings in Greece. [Second Evening]. Sm. fol. [1832]*.

50. The Works of Lord Byron: with his Letters and Journals, and his Life. 17 vols., 8vo. 1832-33.

51. Travels of an Irish Gentleman in search of a Religion. 2 vols., 8vo. 1833.

52. Irish Melodies. Tenth Number. [With Supplement]. Fol. [1834]*.

53. Vocal Miscellany. Number 1. Sm. fol. [1834]*.

54. Vocal Miscellany. Number 2. Sm. fol. [1835]*.

55. The Fudge Family in England. 8vo. 1835.

56. The History of Ireland. First Volume. 8vo. 1835.

57. The History of Ireland. Second Volume. 8vo. 1837.

58. Alciphron, a Poem. 8vo. 1839.

59. The History of Ireland. Third Volume. 8vo. 1840.

60. The Poetical Works of Thomas Moore. Collected by himself. 10 vols., 8 vo. 1840-41.

61. The History of Ireland. Fourth Volume. 8vo. 1846.[19]

[1] I have altered the dates given for the first and second numbers of Irish Melodies in accordance with Mr. Gibson's recent discoveries.—S.G.

[2] Copies of all the editions were exhibited, with the exception of Nos. 8, 11, 13, and 46.

[3] A copy of the second edition, 2 vols. 8vo., 1802, also was shown.

[4] These were only given as a selection.

[5] This edition ends at page 68. Copies of the first reprints, ending at page 51, also were exhibited.

It is to be understood that copies of the Dublin editions and the London editions (both copyright), up to the seventh number, were shown.

[6] A copy is in the British Museum.

[7] This is advertised in William and James Power's trade lists of the period. It is thus referred to in a letter from Moore to his mother, dated "Saturday, May 1811":—"I have been these two or three days past receiving most flattering letters from the persons to whom I sent my Melologue." Kent, in his edition of "The Poetical Works of Thomas Moore," makes the "Melologue" an integral part of the "National Airs," and states the following in reference to the latter:—"Another collection of songs, not unworthy of being placed in companionship with the Irish Melodies, appeared from the hand of Moore in 1815." But the "Melologue" was produced in 1811, as has now been shown, and the first number of the "National Airs" did not make its appearance until 1818, while the last one was only originally published in 1827.

[8] A copy is in the British Museum.

[9] In the London edition the Advertisement is dated "Bury-Street, St. James's, Nov., 1811," whereas in the Dublin edition it is dated "London,—January, 1812."

[10] The London and Dublin editions have each the following "Erratum" annexed to the Advertisement:—"The Reader of the Words is requested to take notice of an alteration (which was made too late to be conveniently printed) in the first verse of the first Song, 'Thro' Erin's Isle'; he will find the verses, in their corrected form, engraved under the Music, Pages 2 and 3."

[11] In the London edition the Advertisement is dated "Mayfield, Ashbourne, March, 1815." In the Dublin edition it has "April" instead of "March."

[12] The London edition imprint reads:—"London, Published by J. Power, 34, Strand." The Dublin edition imprint reads:—"Dublin. Published by W. Power 4 Westmorland St."

[13] The London edition imprint reads:—"London, Published April 23rd, 1818, by J. Power, "34, Strand." The Dublin edition imprint reads:— "Dublin, Published 6th July 1818, by W. Power 4 Westmorland Street."

[14] The London edition imprint reads:—"London, Published October 1st 1818, by J. Power, 34, Strand." The Dublin edition imprint reads:—"Dublin, Published 9th Decr. 1818, by W. Power, 4, Westmorland Street."

[15] The Symphonies and Accompaniments in the London edition are by Henry R. Bishop. Those in the Dublin edition are by Sir John Stevenson.

I exhibited copies of both editions, and read to my audience a telling Advertisement by William Power in the Dublin edition, in which he states that "with *him* originated the idea of uniting the Irish Melodies to characteristic words."

Moore had already entered into a new agreement with James Power, who had not permitted his brother to share in it; and in July 1821, "James Power, of the Strand, London, Music Seller, obtained an injunction to restrain William Power, of Westmorland Street, Dublin, from publishing a pirated edition of the Eighth Number of Moore's Irish Melodies"—*vide* "Notes from the Letters of Thomas Moore to his Music Publisher, James Power," page 88.

[16] The manuscript of the Dedication and the Preface, in Moore's handwriting, also was exhibited. It is the property of Mr. William Swanston.

[17] The copy shown belongs to Mr. Robert May.

[18] A copy of the third edition, 3 vols. 8vo., 1833, was exhibited. I have since obtained a copy of the first edition.

[19] Having spoken for nearly two hours, I found it necessary to refrain from also referring to the following, together with several other works:—

1. Memoirs, Journals, and Correspondence of Thomas Moore. Edited by the Right Honourable Lord John Russell, M.P. 8 vols. 8vo., 1853-56.

2. Notes from the Letters of Thomas Moore to his Music Publisher, James Power (the publication of which was suppressed in London). 8vo. [1854].

3. Prose and Verse, Humorous, Satirical and Sentimental. By Thomas Moore. With suppressed passages from the Memoirs of Lord Byron. Chiefly

from the Author's own Manuscript, and all hitherto inedited and uncollected. 8vo. 1878.

The last-named publication includes the contributions of Moore to the *Edinburgh Review*, between 1814 and 1834.

Milton Keynes UK
Ingram Content Group UK Ltd.
UKHW031048120324
439302UK00006B/494